C.A. Lynch also writes as Carissa Ann Lynch. She is the *USA Today* and *Wall Street Journal* bestselling author of *My Sister Is Missing*, *Without a Trace*, *Like Follow Kill*, *The One Night Stand*, *She Lied She Died*, *Whisper Island*, *The Secrets of Cedar Farm*, the *Flocksdale Files* trilogy, the *Horror High* series, *Searching for Sullivan*, *This Is Not About Love*, *Midnight Moss*, and *Shades and Shadows*. She resides in Floyds Knobs, Indiana, with her partner, children, and collection of books. With a background in psychology, she has always been a little obsessed with the darker areas of the mind.

carissaannlynch.wordpress.com

facebook.com/CarissaAnnLynchauthor
x.com/carissaannlynch
instagram.com/carissaannlynch_thrillers

D1637549

THE TRAITORS

C. A. LYNCH

One More Chapter
a division of HarperCollins*Publishers*
1 London Bridge Street
London SE1 9GF
www.harpercollins.co.uk
HarperCollins*Publishers*
Macken House, 39/40 Mayor Street Upper,
Dublin 1, D01 C9W8, Ireland

This paperback edition 2024
1
First published in Great Britain in ebook format
by HarperCollins*Publishers* 2024
Copyright © C. A. Lynch 2024
C. A. Lynch asserts the moral right to be identified
as the author of this work
A catalogue record of this book is available from the British Library

ISBN: 978-0-00-864394-2

This novel is entirely a work of fiction. The names, characters and incidents portrayed in it are the work of the author's imagination. Any resemblance to actual persons, living or dead, events or localities is entirely coincidental.

Printed and bound in the UK using 100% Renewable Electricity
by CPI Group (UK) Ltd

All rights reserved. No part of this publication may be reproduced, stored in a retrieval system, or transmitted, in any form or by any means, electronic, mechanical, photocopying, recording or otherwise, without the prior permission of the publishers.

To Violet Lynch (my daughter), who created the drawing used
inside this book on my behalf.
To my sons, Tristian and Dexter
To my husband, Shannon
Love you all.

The ninth, the worst circle of the Inferno – Dante intended it for traitors.

Alija Izetbegovic

Prologue

We entered the house on a Friday evening. The sun was still shining; the leaves of the forest glistened with dew. Branches swayed, their bony knuckles beckoning forward, along the trail and through a wooded clearing. They were welcoming us to our new home—our home for one night, at least.

The house itself, a decaying stone monstrosity in the middle of nowhere which was usually an eyesore, looked sweet and serene in the early evening glow. It was surrounded by the hushed sounds of the forest—there was electricity in the air.

Wet tendrils of ivy sparkled like emeralds; crooked shutters and doors looked charming and quaint. The house, only a whisper of what it once was. Locked doors and secrets. A closed-off tower, like something a princess once lived in. And the blood … blood, long dried and faded over the years.

The house appeared harmless, really, like something from a child's fairytale. The steepled roof reaching, reaching … as though it could touch the sky, bringing us closer to heaven itself.

But "the Castle", as the locals called it, was a well-established version of hell. Decades of bad juju were running through its ceilings and walls, leaking down through the planks, permeating the cracked foundation, infecting the ground roots and spreading through the surrounding forest ... eventually poisoning the whole loathsome town of Rock Hill.

We entered the castle, not knowing what lay ahead or what the fates would deal us.

A couple of us were excited.

A few of us were scared.

Most of us were desperate.

But only one was determined ... determined to punish us all.

Chapter One

INVITATIONS

Staci

The letter came on a Tuesday, but it wasn't addressed to me.

I balled up the envelope, folded the letter into a tiny black square, then stuffed both of them in my jean pocket. *For later.*

As I steadied my shaking hands, I watched my best friend, Jan, crossing the street and coming toward where I waited on the front porch for her. Jan was all goose-fleshed and gorgeous—like someone from a different century, she was wearing lacy black gloves and a vintage dress. Her bouncy blonde ponytail swished side to side as she looked left then right, then jogged toward me.

It was a windy, October day—unseasonably warm for this time of year, even by Southern Indiana standards. But there was a blanket of fog over Rock Hill that never seemed to go away, despite the weather.

Jan never arrived by car for our weekly meetings. My best friend wouldn't be caught dead driving, much less riding her roommate's motorcycle, even though we lived in a farming community that was considered "the country" by most anyone's standards. She walked to my house, and she carpooled to work, always harping about the environment and saving money. Jan, the saint. Her goodness was why I'd always loved her, and it's also why she was frequently disappointed by me.

Jan's apartment wasn't far from here. Here: a three-bedroom shotgun that didn't belong to me. I'd been living rent-free for the greater part of the past two years, or "squatting", according to my older—and reasonably responsible—brother, Andrew, and his cunt-ish wife, Phoebe. Between Jan's tiny apartment that she shared with a roommate and my roomy borrowed bedroom crammed with books and dirty clothing, my "space" had the best lighting to make our weekly videos on YouTube.

Truthfully, I hadn't been sure if Jan would show up today. Yet, here she was—floating across the front yard, toting her sparkly black makeup bag, and a few new props for filming.

So, we're going to make new content today, after all. Lately, I wasn't sure where I stood with Jan … and I'd been counting down the days until she ended our "professional" relationship and perhaps our personal, lifelong friendship, too.

"Hey, bestie." Jan took a big step up onto the wooden porch and waited for me to invite her in. Nothing was the same between us—awkward silence and forced niceties, or bickering back and forth about petty stuff that didn't even scratch the surface of the real issue.

The issue: the backlash I'd received from our channel, not Jan. She'd made it very clear that I was the one who fucked up, so that made me the problem, not her...

"Hey to you too, bestie," I deadpanned, taking the bag from her and motioning her to come inside.

The letter in my pocket was temporarily forgotten.

Smells of breakfast lingered; Andrew and Phoebe had left behind a sink full of dishes for me to take care of as they hustled out the door for their day jobs. Andrew worked in construction and Phoebe in finance. Watching them bid their goodbyes in the morning—Andrew in coveralls and her in a slick pantsuit—was always a sight to see. As much as I resented Phoebe for being so unwelcoming toward me, I loved the way she loved my brother. Their life together— the quickly thrown together meals, the messy kitchen, the early bedtimes and sometimes muffled love-making sessions—was something to be admired.

Perhaps I was simply envious of them, and lonely with myself. As a twenty-five-year-old, unemployed college dropout I left a lot to be desired. But it wasn't all my fault and Andrew knew that; that's why he tolerated my living with him and his wife. After years of struggling with depression and anxiety, I'd gotten situated on a good medicine regimen in my late teens. But that all fell apart when our parents died, and I stopped taking the meds correctly. What transpired after their death felt like a blur: the rollercoaster of mania I never wanted to get off of, followed by the lowest, depressing dip of my life and a slew of messes created by my manic-side to clean up...

The money I stole from my job, the failed college courses —it was too much to face afterwards, but also ... too glaring to avoid.

I promised Andrew that my stay with them would be temporary. He brought me home from the hospital with a new list of meds and we came up with a plan.

I was taking the pills, but I hadn't followed through on the rest of it, much to my brother's disappointment.

Instead of looking for a job or trying to meet with advisors to re-enroll at community college, I'd become fixated on mine and Jan's channel, researching unsolved murders or missing persons cases from around the country and shining a light on them for viewers who might have forgotten about the victims involved. Although it technically wasn't a "job", it involved a ton of hours of editing, researching, scripting, and online engagement. Nothing about running our channel was easy.

But that's where Jan came in. Like me, she always had a fixation on the macabre—perhaps it was more me than her, but still ... she took an interest in true crime, too. Jan's primary interest, however, was makeup. Studying to be a beautician, she had bigger dreams than working at our local salon in Rock Hill. Jan wanted to do makeup for the stars, or to become a viral internet sensation, providing tutorials for the masses.

The idea to join our two interests was born from a drunken night, filled with watching too many TikTok and YouTube videos.

"They're all the same. The makeup and the cold cases… what if we combined the two? You talk about the unsolved murders while I do my makeup, probing you with questions and giving a 'face' to the channel itself?" Jan said.

It seemed kind of silly, but it didn't take long for me to discover that it wasn't a totally novel idea. There were other channels, some semi-successful, that joined makeup art with story time. But Jan and I could do it better, or we at least were determined to try.

Now, a little over a year after starting, we were a quarter of a way to a million subscribers.

"Free makeup samples and pepper spray gadgets aren't going to pay the bills, Staci," Phoebe said. Her words cut like a knife over dinner, as I'd tried to share the news of our channel's growth with my brother.

I'd looked to Andrew for reassurance then, the way I had when we were younger, and I needed him for back-up…but my brother had simply winced when Phoebe said that and went back to stirring food around on his plate.

His silence hurt me fiercely. And I hadn't mentioned the channel since that encounter … although I knew that both Andrew and Phoebe were aware of it; after all, they had both subscribed.

"Are Andrew and Phoebe here?" Jan asked, pausing in

the kitchen to look around. Despite this morning's mess, the kitchen was the nicest room in the house. My brother had always loved cooking and his passion was evident in the glass-fronted cabinets, stainless-steel appliances, and top-of-the-line cooking gadgets arranged on its granite countertops. Sometime today, before my brother and sister-in-law were due to arrive home, I'd scrub every dish and spit shine the counters until they were gleaming.

Jan knew they weren't home; they were never here when we did our filming in the daytime, but I supposed she was trying to fill the space with small-talk, ease some of the tension that had been building between us for the last few weeks.

"No, they're both at work. Come on." I led her down a narrow, dark hallway filled with paneled walls and store-bought photos, and opened the door to my bedroom. I'd made an effort this morning, making my bed. Tucking in the corners all neat. And I'd scooted my pile of laundry into the closet and closed the door. It wasn't that I minded doing laundry; it was just difficult to work around Andrew and Phoebe's wash times without irritating them, and Andrew had a lifelong habit of leaving clothes in the dryer for weeks. I would have offered to fold his clothes, but I got the impression that my sister-in-law wouldn't like me invading her privacy and touching all her nice things.

My bedroom was decent-sized, with old-fashioned green and yellow flowered wallpaper, a couple of floor-to-ceiling windows, and lots of natural lighting. When we first started the channel, I'd pushed the small twin bed in the corner, and centered the large vanity table and props we used in the middle of the room. This gave us plenty of space in the center for filming, our chairs on either side of the vanity, which also functioned as my desk, and kept my bed and personal items out of view from the cameras.

I placed Jan's makeup bag on the long counter of the vanity for her, next to the antique hand mirrors and combs we'd picked out from a thrift store together when we first got started with the channel. Things were exciting then, every new subscriber and minor sponsor a huge deal for us. Every small milestone felt like one worth celebrating...

But despite our continued channel growth, we didn't have much to celebrate lately. And that was all my fault.

"What case are we doing today? I've forgotten," Jan murmured, lining up three different makeup brushes side by side and digging through her bag for eyeshadow palettes. She usually tried to theme her makeup in a way that fit the case: sometimes dark and macabre, but sometimes softer blues or greens, or rich browns, to match the landscape or towns in which the crimes we were discussing took place.

I felt a twinge of annoyance. Jan not knowing what story we were doing was so typical ... and a perfect example of why she didn't deserve to know about the letter. Sure, her makeup tutorials were entertaining to some, but it was my hard work behind the scenes, hours' worth of researching, digging for new information, and practicing my lines, which made up the crux of our channel. I'd tried to get her more involved in the research side of things, but she only seemed interested in decorating her face and chatting with commenters online these days.

"The Ronnie Nichols case," I said, taking a seat on the edge of the bed and giving her some space to set up. I watched her line up the tubes of concealer and open a long container of false eyelashes, her perfectly manicured nails moving with practice and precision. Jan was good at what she did, and I respected that, but the cases were supposed to be central to our story. Most importantly, the victims we discussed were supposed to take center stage. And I could have used her help, and more interest, when it came to working through the details involved during the pre-filming stage.

I cleared my throat. I should have been setting up the video equipment while she worked on makeup, but I wanted her to remember the importance of Ronnie's case. "Let me refresh your memory. Ronnie is the girl who went missing in Franklin, Missouri after wandering off a local bike trail with her crummy boyfriend and his creepy friends. I told you about it a few weeks ago."

Cases like Ronnie's were a dime a dozen; girls and women went missing every day, and so many were never seen or heard from again.

Jan was still prepping her utensils, but I could see the thoughtful expression on her face as she considered my words. She was holding something back.

"If you have something to say, just say it," I said, crossing my arms over my chest.

Jan sighed and turned around, leaning casually against

the vanity desk. "Look, Staci. I love you. But what happened with the Stevens case can't happen with this one, too. You just called the boyfriend and his friends creepy, but they were never charged with her abduction or murder. It's okay to state your opinion. Our viewers love that. But you can't go spewing stuff and pretending it's straight facts again. Or worse, creating your own 'facts' out of thin air…" Jan mimicked quotation marks in the air when she said the word "facts", and sighed deeply. "We're under too big of a microscope now. You know that, don't you?"

So, we're finally going to discuss this. Good.

Jan was referring to a case we covered back in August. It was the end of summer, sticky hot, and miserable. And reading about the Stevens case made my blood feel like it was boiling, literally. Kacey Stevens was a small-town girl from a no-name town with a poor, shitty family. Even before she went missing, her life was in the pits. Some drug peddling, some prostitution, but Kacey was finally getting her life on track, working on her GED and she'd even hooked her first real boyfriend…a "nice boy", as they liked to call boys like him in the papers. A boy with a toothpaste smile and a good family. Even though they found some signs of blood and a struggle in the boyfriend's car, after a road trip, there was never enough to charge him with kidnapping, much less murder. Furthermore, the searches for Kacey were short and unsuccessful, and her body was never found.

Kacey's case wasn't so dissimilar from others we'd worked on in the past. But what struck me so deeply about it was the fact that it got so little coverage in the news. Kacey was described by some as a "homely-looking" girl, and she was quite a bit overweight. I saw cases of pretty girls all over the news every day; some of those girls were poor no-names like Kacey, but because they were eye-catching with their looks, those cases went viral and the media pushed local authorities to search better, fight harder for justice...

Nobody was fighting for Kacey, because her face simply wasn't memorable enough by today's standards. Girls like Kacey don't light up rooms when they walk inside them. And neither do girls like me.

So, maybe that's why the Stevens hit me so hard. And why I chose to jeopardize everything I'd worked for because of it.

I had a wild idea—to create my own audio recording. An "anonymous source" sent it to us—possible "proof" of the boyfriend discussing the crime with a fellow classmate. When we posted the audio submission, it wasn't a lie exactly—I just forgot to mention that I was the "source", and that I'd created the recording myself using easy-to-download apps and some software. Anonymous sources lie all the time; so, who cares if that source was me?

But I received a humbling lesson with the Stevens case—for every armchair detective out there like me, there's a dozen more where that came from...

And once the audio clip went completely viral, we received calls from the Mount Zion police department and online analysts. The clip was played and analyzed hundreds of thousands of times; and since it was fake, it was quickly debunked. I knew it would be, but not so quickly. Apparently, piecing together your own sounds from the internet to form a new 'unique' clip, was not a novel idea either.

"We're lucky that no one is pressing charges, Staci," Jan said, snapping her fingers in the air to get my attention.

"I know and I'm sorry. It was so wrong of me to do—"

"I just don't understand what you were thinking!" Jan pushed off the desk and started pacing back and forth in front of me like an angry schoolmarm. "You had to know that the clip would get looked into ... that your lie would be uncovered. Did you really think the police would charge that boy without a body and all because some stupid YouTuber with an amateur audio file said so?!"

I flinched. "No, of course I knew they wouldn't. And yes, I know I made a mistake. A huge one. But has it ever occurred to you that I did it for the right reasons? That my heart was in the right place..."

"Nothing you're saying is making any sense!" Jan growled. She turned back toward her station but instead of organizing her makeup utensils, she started putting them away.

So, we're finally done. I knew this day was coming ... I just didn't expect it to be today.

"Hear me out. I thought I was doing something noble, okay? It's not fair, the way the media treats victims. If they're not the right age or color, or they don't look Instagram-worthy in their missing photos, then nobody gives a damn…" I could hear the shake in my voice, feel the flushing heat of tears coming. "Look, Jan. Please don't go. I made up the clip for one simple reason. I knew it would gain us more attention and ultimately, bring more media interest to Kacey's case. I don't want her to get swallowed up in the missing case files of troubled girls. And I was willing to do whatever it took to bring more attention to it, and up the pressure on those detectives in charge of finding her! Even if it meant being dishonest … even if it meant risking it all…"

Jan zipped her bag and when she turned around to look at me, her face was a mask of pure disdain. "Well, we lost nearly a third of our subscribers over it and all of our credibility. The research we do means nothing if it isn't real."

"The research I do," I corrected her. "You just paint your face."

Now it was Jan's turn to look affronted. "Yeah, well, I have a fucking job, Staci. I don't have as much time as you do to dedicate to this channel. I wish I didn't have to work. Wouldn't that be nice? You ought to try getting a job yourself. Stop feeling sorry for yourself and blaming it on your mental illness. Do something with your life! This can't be all of it … all you want…" Jan motioned toward the walls and the small bed in the corner. I shrunk back from her, shocked by her callous words and demeanor. Jan, the saint, finally unpinning her holy veil…

"Fuck you, Jan. Go back to your job and I'll go back to working on these cases by myself like I originally intended..." I said, turning my back to her so she wouldn't see the crumpled look on my face.

Without another word, she stormed out of my bedroom and stomped back down the hall. Moments later, I winced at the sound of the front door slamming.

Closing my eyes and rubbing my temples, I tried to convince myself that I was right, and Jan was wrong. But so much of what she'd said was true. I did jeopardize our research on the case, and I did it behind her back, costing us a ton of credibility and work we'd put into this channel. I also used my disorder as a crutch at times; there was some truth to that as well.

And she accused me of telling lies ... that part is certainly true.

I sat down hard on the bed, making the worn-out springs groan in protest, and I pulled the covers over my legs.

I certainly am a liar for hiding the letter from her today...

But since Jan was no longer committed to the channel, then the letter shouldn't matter to her anyway. Slowly, I wiped the tears from my cheeks and pulled out the small letter I'd hidden in my pocket earlier.

For the hundredth time this morning, I reread the tiny gold printed letters:

You are cordially invited to Beechwood Castle on November 9th, 2023 for a night you'll never forget...

Even though I was an embarrassment to my family and

a disappointment to my viewers and friends, the opportunity this letter presented was one small flicker of hope in the dimming cave of my existence.

Shortly after our channel grew in popularity and we started receiving correspondence from viewers, I'd agreed to take charge of our PO box and sort through all correspondence weekly on mine and Jan's behalf. Most of the letters we received were compliments or complaints; sometimes they were suggestions or requests for us to cover specific cases. But this letter—*this letter*—finding it in the stack of mail was like Charlie finding the golden ticket to enter the chocolate factory.

Like Grandpa Joe, I was lying in bed, holding a tiny ticket of hope. This invitation could change everything … not only for my financial future, but for my channel and the sake of all future cold cases I wished to pursue.

The biggest local true crime case of my lifetime happened at the place where I was invited: Beechwood Castle. Not only would I now have an opportunity to experience the scene myself, but if I made it through the whole night—and there was no doubt about it, *I would make it*—then I'd walk away with enough money to get out from under my brother and sister-in-law and make a real name for myself online.

I should call Jan right now and tell her. After all, her name was in the letter.

Showing her the letter would be like a peace offering…

But I was done making peace for now.

It's every man or woman for themselves.

I tucked the letter inside my nightstand, then set up for today's video. I was prepared to cover the Ronnie Nichols case, but that would have to be put on hold for a little while.

My hair was messy and uncombed, and I wasn't wearing any makeup, but none of that mattered anymore. I pressed the record button and took my seat, alone, at the vanity table. I'd spent the morning thinking about what I would say when the moment came, and that moment was now. But I had nothing specific planned. No script.

Sometimes it's best to just go rogue.

"Hello to all my viewers. It's me, your host, Stabby Staci," I said, staring boldly into the lens. "I know that I usually say, 'Hello, beautiful people' when I begin a video, but that changes now. Being beautiful doesn't make you good or worthy. And every woman out there, no matter how pretty, worthy, or kind, deserves to be found when she goes missing. I know what I did was wrong, y'all I'm not here today to justify those actions. But I would like to take a couple minutes to explain why I did what I did. I thought that if I created enough interest with the fake audio clip, then maybe the internet would help me find Kacey. As women, we spend so much time worrying about how we look—hell, up until today, I had an assistant doing her makeup on the show. But that all ends now, too. Jan will no longer be a part of this channel, and I'm sorry if that upsets some of you. But the truth is … no matter how much we try to dress it up and put a pretty spin on tragedy, there's nothing beautiful about missing or dead women. Again, I'm sorry for what I did. My intentions were pure, but I made a massive mistake. I want to apologize to Kacey, wherever she is. As well as Kacey's family and friends, and to the Mount Zion police department. Viewers, I must certainly apologize to you. You trusted me, and I failed you. I would understand if you stopped watching my videos … but now I'm here today, asking you to stick around. If only for a little while longer, I need you all to hang in there and give me another chance. Because something huge has happened. And it's happened to me. Have you all heard of the Castle Mass Murder that happened in Rock Hill in 1996? Well, that happened only a few miles away from where I live. The Beechwood Castle grounds have been locked down since the nineties, well-gated by an electric fence and unpassable thickets and pines. But, last week, there was an announcement all over the news and social media. Some of you might have seen it, but most of you, probably not. It's mostly been a big story around here, in my own small local community. After all these years, someone has purchased the property. I don't know who it is, but this 'someone' is opening up the doors of the castle on November 9th and letting six guests inside. This was a horrific case, one that was never solved. A local, troubled man named Bobby Reeks was suspected of committing the crime, but I don't believe that. There's not enough evidence to prove he was the killer, and he's no longer alive to defend himself. Now, six people will get a chance to go inside it. They will also be competing for money."

I took a deep breath, adrenaline soaring through my veins. I wasn't live, but I might as well have been.

"Viewers … one of those six is me. I'm going to Beechwood Castle for one night, and one night only. And sure, I'd love to win the money. But, most importantly, I want to share that experience with all of you, as much as they will permit, and I want to find out who killed those innocent teenagers back in 1996."

I stood up behind the desk and placed my palms flat on the surface, leaning my face closer to the lens.

"Will you all stand by me for a little while longer? I need this chance to redeem myself, and I'm determined to do just that. I will make it up to all of you, at any cost."

Chapter Two

Lolly

On the day my invitation to Beechwood Castle arrived, I wasn't a bit surprised. Of course I'd been invited to that crumbling, cursed, piece-of-shit heap in the woods. It wouldn't be a good PR stunt without me included, I'd thought, angrily ripping the invitation to shreds and shoving it down so deep in the trashcan that the bits got covered in glops of tuna and canned corn.

But now, one week later, the scratchy black letters on the invitation were still seared into my brain.

You are cordially invited to Beechwood Castle on November 9th, 2023, for a night you'll never forget … its new owner plans to reinvigorate the property, but before they do, they're offering you, and five others, an enthralling opportunity! You are invited to stay one night, as our guest. If you follow the rules and complete the night, you will receive your one-sixth share of one million dollars. If you plan to accept this challenge, please respond, in writing and postmarked by November 1st to the PO Box listed below. Upon acceptance, you will receive a packet filled with more detailed documents. See you soon.

Today is October 31st, only one day before the designated response date.

Such bullshit: the invitation written out like it was some sort of perverse theater—act one of an amateur play or the intro to a cringey murder-mystery videogame.

Well, they could kiss my ass—whoever this anonymous Willy Wonka asshole happened to be.

There wasn't a chance in hell I was going, but I couldn't help wondering who the other five invitees were, and what the exact motivations of the event planner were.

What did they hope to gain from my presence there? Notoriety? More answers about what happened all those years ago…?

I had no doubt this stunt and the invitations were related to the mass murder, but why, exactly? Was it because of the thirty-year anniversary of the tragedy? But no, that was still a few years away… Did they plan to film the invitees, make it some sort of documentary? Was the whole thing supposed to be centered around me?

Imagining the headlines, I stood at the kitchen counter, staring across the stretch of cornfields behind my childhood home as the sun settled behind the clouds and the moon made its first nightly appearance. Our closest neighbor was a half mile away, but I could still see the soft, haunting glow of his jack-o-lanterns, and the perfect, zig-zag rows cut through the cornfield that he set up every year for the local kids.

Halloween. What an awful day.

Sadie was due back in a couple hours; my thirteen-year-old daughter had attended her first school dance. Too old now for trick-or-treating, she'd dressed up in an elaborate Shrek costume (her best friend Jamie went as Donkey), and she'd caught a ride to the dance with her best friend's mom.

I knew I shouldn't be worried. Sadie was young and impulsive at times, like all young kids can be, but she had a good head on her shoulders. She didn't drink or smoke or do any of the other reckless things I was doing when I was her age. At her age, I would have chosen a slutty Halloween costume, in an attempt to gain attention from boys. But not Sadie—she was funny and kind, and always focused on her own inner sanctum. She had the sort of confidence that I admired, and that I wish I had had a tiny sliver of when I was that age…

Thirteen.

Hard to believe that's the age I was when I last entered Beechwood Castle. Less of a castle and more of a broken-down palace of crumbling pillars and rot-ridden walls, the property had been abandoned and grim even back then, twenty-seven years ago. It looked medieval with its tower and battlements, but it was actually built after the Civil War, by a group of brothers, all Union soldiers, to protect their families from another possible uprising in the South.

The place had been renovated and resold in the early twentieth century, used for multiple purposes, including a children's orphanage at one time, and a refuge for the homeless during the Great Depression.

Some had even speculated that it had been around longer than that—there were stories when I was a child, kids calling it the "Witch's Castle". A wicked place full of vampires and occultists, and eventually even Satanists. But most of those stories were more myth than legend—an attempt by local adults to keep teenagers away from the thorny patch of forest and the dangerous rumbled house in the woods.

But those tall tales didn't serve as a deterrent; in fact, they were the reason we went there, looking for adventure, and sometimes, trouble.

Over the years, I'd done a little online research on the castle, usually late at night when I couldn't sleep. But mostly, I tried not to think about that hellish place at all. No matter what it was before, or what it became after, it would always be the place where my friends were brutally murdered.

Nothing will ever change that fact. And no amount of restoration or "breathing new life" into the forty-acre wooded property and that revolting "castle", would change what happened there.

The people of Rock Hill would certainly never forget, and neither would I.

Through the windows, I watched a ghoulish group of children in the encroaching dark—probably aged nine or ten years old, followed closely by their parents—skipping toward my tiny farmhouse.

Trick or treat. There will be neither of those here. Not this year, nor the next. Sorry kids…

I made no moves toward the door; the porchlight was off—the universal sign for "go away" on Halloween night. I heard the stomp of tiny feet on the small porch anyway, and then the shouting of adult voices in the street. "The lights aren't on! Come back, you guys! We never go to that house anyway."

I closed my eyes and held my breath, waiting for them to leave.

Nobody came to this house, but it wasn't the house itself they wished to avoid. It was the sad, haunting girl—a woman, now—who was known for one thing, and one thing only, in the town of Rock Hill. I was the final girl of the Beechwood Castle Massacre. The only one to survive that horrible night in 1996, when three of my friends were savagely slaughtered by a lunatic with an ax.

You'd think being a survivor would have made me popular. Perhaps, in a different era, the TikTok story time generation … perhaps then, it would have. But back then, on the heels of the eighties' Satanic Panic phase, there were questions and rumors about me that ran amok. *What were they doing out there anyway? Some sort of Satanic ritual in the woods…? Was there really a killer out there with them, or could Lolly Andrews be the one who committed those heinous deeds herself? Why did the killer leave her alive? Was she involved in the murders, some sort of accomplice? Or was she just a coward—*

hiding away, leaving her friends to fend for themselves from an ax-wielding psycho in the woods? Or worse, could she be the psycho killer herself?

The townspeople had their fun and spread their gossip, and eventually it all died down. But still, the stories had a way of cropping back up from time to time. Especially now, with the thirty-year anniversary only a few years off. And ever since that god awful radio and newspaper announcement about the reopening of the castle and the six anonymous, randomly chosen invitees, the stirrings had begun again. Newspapers and crime bloggers had tried to reach out—but just like all those years ago, I'd given no comment.

I had nothing left to say about that night. Back then, I'd told the police everything that I knew, which honestly, was painfully little.

The bottle of bourbon was tucked away in the cabinet over the fridge. I used a chair to reach it, then took out a small tumbler from the cabinet and poured a glass. The last thing I wanted to do was get drunk before Sadie returned home, especially if I had to interact with her friend Jamie's mother at drop-off. But I needed a little something … something to take the edge off, as those words played through my mind again and again—*if you follow the rules and complete the night, you will receive your one-sixth share of one million dollars.*

Sure, the money was tempting. I'd never planned on staying in Rock Hill, especially after the tragedy. But then my mother had died, and I'd become pregnant with Sadie, and then Dad's dementia hit. I was stuck here with the little money I earned from my job at Home Depot and whatever side hustle I could find. Raising a teenager and paying a mortgage wasn't cheap, and now that Dad's dementia was worsening, assisted living and the costs associated with it was a very real possibility, and a constant niggling source of concern for me.

But no amount of money would ever be enough to make me go back there. To make me put my own tragedy and the deaths of my friends on display for others, a circus just to earn a bit of extra cash. Because it was undoubtedly some sort of media stunt, focused on the murders—of that, I had no doubt.

I took a small sip of the bourbon and opened my phone's calculator app. It wouldn't hurt to do the math, though. A million dollars divided by six...

I flinched at the number on the screen. *A million dollars divided six ways is 166, 666 dollars. And 66 cents.*

"Well, if that's not a bad omen then I don't know what is," I muttered into my glass, before swallowing the entire contents in one long swig.

Placing the glass in the sink for washing later, I made my way down the hallway to the bathroom, eager to brush my teeth and use mouthwash before Sadie got back.

But before I could reach the bathroom, my father rounded the corner, giving me a start. He was dressed in a pajama top, but he wasn't wearing any pants.

"Dad! What are you doing up?"

I'd put him to bed an hour ago, after making sure he

took his meds properly and that he had everything he needed for bed—his glass of water and his paperback, the same book he'd been reading for ages.

"Well, I'll tell you what I'm doing, missy! Can't a man have a little private time, without your hooligan friends banging down my door at all hours of the night? I heard them out there. That girl, Monica … I knew her mom once, you know. If the daughter is anything like the mother, then you need to stay the hell away from her. And those boys she runs around with, too!"

"Dad." Gently, I took him by the elbow and tried to lead him back to bed.

"Don't touch me, Lolly! I know what you've been up to. Nothing good, that's for sure! This is my house, and you will respect my rules!"

I stepped back from my father, giving him space. Although his dementia often made him irritable, he'd only become combative once. But still—it was enough to teach me a lesson. To create space when he was mad. Especially when he thought I was still that daughter, the wild teenager, whose friends woke him up late in the evenings. The girl who got in trouble often.

I'd read enough about dementia and talked to enough of Dad's doctors and nurses to know that I wasn't supposed to argue with him, when it came to his reality. But, perhaps, it was my own selfishness that forced out the words:

"Actually, Dad, this is my house now. I pay the mortgage every month, and I'm forty-three years old. Old enough to make my own choices, and old enough to tell you to back off. And my friends? My friends are all dead, Dad. Including Monica, who you like to speak so fondly of. My friends were murdered nearly thirty years ago. But you didn't seem to care much then, so you probably don't now either."

My father stumbled over his own feet, his face a twisted mask of confusion. I felt a twinge of guilt, but less than I probably should have.

"Your mother ... where's your mother? I need her, Lolly. Please."

I was cruel, but not that cruel. I'd told him before that Mom was dead, dead and gone for more than two decades, in fact. But I didn't have the heart tonight.

"She's on her way home, Dad. Why don't you go wait for her in bed?"

I took him by the arm again, eyes avoiding his bare lower half, and I led him slowly back through the hallway, into the main bedroom of the house. It should have rightfully been my bedroom, but I'd let Dad move into it when he became sick and couldn't live on his own anymore. Sadie and I shared the small bedroom down the hall, which surprisingly, she didn't seem to mind. Sharing a room with your mom is cool when you're a kid—two-person slumber parties and late-night cuddles—but Sadie was a teenager now, her own person. She needed her space. And frankly, I needed mine.

Dad's confusion and agitation was worsening by the day, and it was only a matter of time before assisted living was a real and unavoidable option to be considered.

But affording it on my small salary was going to be nearly impossible.

After helping my father into bed and tucking the blanket up to his chin, I made my way back to the kitchen to console myself with a new glass of bourbon.

Taking care of sick parents is hard on anyone. It's the circle of life, they say. Your parents raise you and care for you, and then later in life, there's a good chance they'll need you to return the favor. But nobody tells you how to deal with it when your relationship with them is already strained. My father didn't coddle or comfort me as a child. In fact, most of my memories of him were bad. His anger, the drinking, the way he treated mom...

There was a part of me, the part of me I got from my mother, that wanted to play the role of dutiful daughter and give my father the most considerate and loving care possible. After all, his dementia wasn't his fault. He didn't ask for this.

But there was another part, that sad child and that angsty teen, that couldn't let myself care as much as I should. When he lashed out in anger or confusion, it just felt like normal behavior to me. And as a grown woman, struggling to raise another girl into a woman, I grew frustrated easily, and often lashed right back at him.

Leaning against the counter, I took a few small sips of the woodsy drink, letting it warm my chest. These days, I tried to take comfort in the small things—a warm drink, a good book, a cozy nap stolen during the day.

Suddenly, I heard the thump of feet on the wooden

boards outside again. This time, too heavy to be the small, mistaken feet of trick-or-treaters. And it was too early for Sadie to be home; plus, I hadn't heard the sounds of Mrs. Reynolds' rumbly truck in the driveway.

Tilting my head to the side, I listened. Waited for the doorbell to ring. Perhaps it was teenagers out hunting candy; some of the kids nowadays looked like grown men and women to me.

But there was nothing. No knocks or bells.

I washed my glass in the sink and loaded it in the dishwasher with the other one, then went to the front door and flipped the porch light on for Sadie's return. That's when I saw it through the sliver of glass on the front door— a large envelope on the front porch, sitting on the welcome mat.

I wasn't expecting an Amazon or UPS delivery, but sometimes I ordered stuff late at night and then forgot about it until it showed up days later…

I unlatched the deadbolt and lock, then reached out and picked it up. I looked left and right down the now-deserted street. No one.

A gust of wind, icy and sharp, came blowing through, sending waves of chills down my spine.

I slammed the door and locked it back, returning to the kitchen and placing the package on the dinette table.

The thin package had no return address.

Could this be from the same assholes who sent the invitation? I hadn't accepted their invitation, so why would they send me more documents unasked?

Clenching my teeth in irritation, I ripped open the top of the package and turned it over. Eight wispy pieces of paper came falling out. Carefully, I spread them out, one by one, then stood there, frozen in horror with a hand over my mouth.

There were eight drawings, all made with a childish hand. Most seemed innocent, others looked more macabre. But it wasn't the drawings themselves that shook me, it was the artist I knew too well and the place where these drawings had come from that chilled me...

As a young kid and teenager, I'd always carried around notebooks and paper to sketch with. It didn't matter what I was doing, if I had a free moment, I slid one of them out and started scribbling away. I hadn't drawn anything in decades, but instantly, I recognized my own childlike handiwork. After all, I'd drawn these same images over and over again...

The last time I saw these drawings was the last night I held my favorite green sketchbook in my hands. The night that my friends were murdered, that infamous night at Beechwood Castle.

I'd left the notebook behind that night, and I didn't think about it for months, not until long after the shock of the murders. I waited for the cops to bring it back to me, or to question me about my strange artwork, the way some of my teachers did at school. But no one ever brought it back; over time, I'd forgotten about it, considering it one small thing I'd lost on a night filled with many losses.

All I knew was that whoever dropped off these pages

must have had access to my old sketchbook. The pages looked worn and torn, as though someone had haphazardly yanked them out of the book and saved them for later.

My head spinning, I poured myself a third glass of bourbon, then took a seat at the table to study the drawings more closely.

Even though they were created by my own hand, or at least appeared to be, I couldn't help feeling unsettled by them. But mostly, I couldn't understand who would have left these for me, and how they ended up with the drawings in the first place...

Chapter Three

Cornelius

"Cornelius Jones, your breakfast is ready! I've called for you, like, eighty times!"

Cornelius Jones. Even first thing in the morning, before I open my eyes, I'm reminded of my own personal hell—the one I'm stuck in and can't get out of.

This December, it will be ten years since I married my wife. Patricia's brashness and habit of calling me pet names, as well as shouting out my full name when she's serious, used to be qualities that I found cute and silly about her.

But now, all of those glowing, girlish qualities I used to love had dried up, or gone sour. It didn't help that there was a truly serious edge to her voice these days when she shouted, if not the downright taste of pure hatred flowing from her tongue.

On the upper level of our swanky townhouse, I could hear Patricia doing the same routine with our twin boys— "Michael and Christopher Jones! Time to get ready for school!"

Groaning, I shoved aside pillows and blankets, and looked at the empty side that Patricia used to sleep on beside me. It had been nearly two months now since she'd taken the guest room. I'd offered to take it myself, of course; I was capable of being a gentleman when I wanted to be. But she'd refused: "Oh no, I wouldn't dare think of inconveniencing my brilliant architect husband, Cornelius Jones," she had said, flashing me with an evil grin that she seemed to relish before carrying off her own set of extra blankets and pillows from our bedroom closet.

I ran my fingers through my brown, graying hair, then stood up and began getting dressed for the day. Slacks and a decent polo—that was the plan. That was the plan every day, these days, as I spent my mornings shuffling around Rock Hill, job hunting.

But I had no clean polos hanging up. I dug around the bottom of the closet and opened a few drawers. No polos. That was another thing that had changed recently—Patricia had stopped washing my clothes.

Each day, I headed out right after breakfast for a day of knocking on doors and filling out job applications. But, in reality, I only spent a short while each morning looking; instead, I'd park somewhere safe and quiet in my car, drink a couple cups of strong coffee, then slowly make the drive back to our townhouse, praying Patricia had left for Rock Hill Elementary, the place where she spent her days teaching bright-eyed kindergarteners, who probably enjoyed her high-pitched voice and her put-on smile.

I hadn't liked my wife in a while. And now, finally, the feeling seemed to be mutual.

Sure, I loved her once. She was the mother to our two boys and my first real love after high school. Motherhood had suited her well, perhaps too well. Because, frankly, she'd turned into a dullard after the boys were born, spending all her focus and attention on them. Letting herself go...

I waited until I heard the sounds of galloping, the boys wrestling each other and racing down the steps from their bedroom, each boy always trying to be first in line for breakfast. As soon as I knew the boys were there to create a buffer between Patricia and me, I emerged with a phony smile in a crinkled sweater, and I entered the kitchen, kissing first Patricia (who flinched) and then both boys (who also flinched).

"Looks yummy," I said to my wife, taking my seat at the head of the table. She refused to look at me, treating me like a ghost, as she moved from plate to plate, filling each with scrambled eggs, fried potatoes, and wheat toast.

I noticed that she filled my plate last—another new change from Patricia. Another small way of getting back at me for what I'd done.

Head tucked down, I dug into my eggs and potatoes,

barely tasting the food. The boys were chatting about their latest school project and arguing over their current favorite Roblox game, but I was mostly tuning them out. As usual, Patricia was the dutiful mother, leaning into every word they said and responding as though she were the same age as them, in that patronizing voice I'd grown to hate.

We used to be good together. Fun, sexy … adventurous. But now we were boring old parents. And worse, now Patricia hated me.

Two months had passed since "the incident" (that was what Patricia liked to call it; never willing to discuss the actual details) – "the incident" being my very public arrest at our local JayC food store and the charges brought against me. With the help of my lawyer, I pled down quickly, receiving a misdemeanor "Lewd Conduct" charge, a slap on the wrist essentially, and thirty-six hours of community service, that I completed within the first few weeks (at Patricia's insistence, of course).

There are few things worse that you can do to Patricia than causing embarrassment. She had nearly fainted that day in the store as they carted me off; I'll never forget her face—cranberry red, then sickly white. There were rumors that she fainted right there in the store afterwards, but Patricia claims those are untrue.

The worst part of it all, besides my wife's disgust and hatred, was the fact that I lost my job.

Tens of thousands of dollars in student loan debt was bad enough; but losing my first "real" job relating to my skill—an architect's apprentice—was devastating for my career. And my wallet.

While I'd been hunting for other similar jobs, Patricia had encouraged me to just "take what you can get because we need the money". But I didn't go to school for all that time, just to go backwards now.

The whole "incident" was blown out of proportion, anyway. Yes, I was peeping into one of my client's bedrooms. And yes, my pants were around my ankles.

But I wasn't trying to expose myself, and it's not like I planned on raping her.

There were all these tiny scraps of info, like the declaration of facts they presented in court, and those scraps were used to build a story around them—Cornelius, the pervert. Cornelius, the creepy sex offender.

God forbid society allowed me to just be a man.

I'd lucked out by avoiding the sex offender registry. If I'd had to put my face on that registry and be plastered all over the internet, Patricia would have left me for good.

Some days I wondered why she hadn't left yet. But then I remembered—Patricia was all about appearances. She had to decide between two bad outcomes—leave me and endure the embarrassment and struggle of being a single mother, and ultimately, losing our house and most of the nice things we own. Or stay with me and endure the embarrassment of being married to a pervert.

For now, Cornelius the Pervert was where she was leaning.

"Thanks for breakfast. I'm heading out. I got a lead on a new job site that's looking for someone with my skill set," I told her, dumping my plate in the sink.

If Patricia heard me, she pretended not to. I kissed the boys on the top of their soft, blonde heads, smiled at my annoying wife, and headed out the front door.

In the driver's seat of my Mustang—a car I'd splurged on with some of my extra student loan money before "the incident"—I felt the tension ease from my shoulders and my lungs expand in my chest. Lately, I couldn't stand being in that house. Some days, I fantasized about leaving it all ... getting in the car and just driving and driving, starting a new life somewhere else, where no one knew my name or the stupid crime I was forced into signing a plea deal for.

But leaving the boys ... I wasn't sure if that were something I could do yet.

I'd been searching online for places I could go, maybe somewhere on the beach. And eventually, after the divorce was final, I could see the boys during the summer, or something.

But now I had a new opportunity—a small speck of hope.

I pulled out of the driveway, but instead of heading into town, I drove toward the local park. It was only a few miles from our house, so minutes later, I was parking in a gravel lot that overlooked a spread of grass filled with monkey bars, plastic slides, and swing sets.

The park was empty, as it usually was this time of day.

From the glove box, I took out a small manilla envelope and removed the cardboard letter from inside.

I meant to tell Patricia about the invitation. But every time I asked to talk to her, or tried to approach her after the boys went to bed, she gave me the cold shoulder. Last night, I'd gone to the spare bedroom shortly after the boys went to sleep, but the door was locked. I knocked several times, but no answer.

I know she was pretending to be asleep because I saw that she was active on Facebook.

What a bitch.

Truthfully, it was her own fault that I hadn't told her about the invitation. Perhaps I wouldn't tell her at all. She'd wake up next week to find my bed—*our* bed—empty, and then she would be left to worry about where I'd gone, and who I was with…

With my fingertips, I traced the letters of the invitation. They were fancy and bold, like it was written for someone special.

At least someone still thinks I'm important…

You are cordially invited to Beechwood Castle on November 9th, 2023, for a night you'll never forget…

When I heard the news a few weeks ago about the Beechwood property getting a new owner, I'd been curious about who it was. In the small amount of time I'd worked for the architect, Greg Bronin, I'd met many local real estate developers and builders in our area. But no one had talked about the Beechwood property in years, and I had no idea who the new owner might be.

It had crossed my mind—how cool it would be to get picked—but I'd assumed they'd bring in fake actors from big states, like New York or California, make it some sort of stupid reality TV show…

But now that I knew I'd been chosen, the wheels were turning … how incredible would it be to get inside the "castle"? A chance to meet a new builder or developer in the area. *Hell, it's possible he chose me exactly because of who I am, and he admires my work.*

Beechwood "Castle" was less of a castle, and more of a manor with a tower and battlements. Last I'd heard, it was crumbling to pieces. But it was still an incredible piece of architecture and history, and I couldn't wait to get inside it.

From what I'd read, it was constructed with stone, iron, and tin. Nothing in our area was built with that kind of fortification. How amazing (and fun!) would it be to restore the "castle" to its former glory? And even if the owner had plans of tearing it down and building a community of McMansions, I could get on board with that too.

I'll do anything to secure a paycheck and gain some dignity back…

Even if a new job didn't come out of the whole experience, then at least I could collect the prize money. Money like that, over a 100k … it would be enough to sneak off to Florida or South Carolina, maybe, start my life over again, in a place where I wasn't ridiculed, shunned, or hated. In a place that didn't include my annoying bitch of a wife.

The thought of having all that money in my hands, and a possible job too, gave me an instant boner. I glanced around the park hurriedly, and made sure I was alone. Then I slid my pants and underwear down and reached for the tube of lotion that I kept under the driver's seat.

Chapter Four

Penelope

"**E**veryone hates me. Just say it. You used to be good at shooting the shit, Liz … you're losing your touch!" I shouted into the phone at my agent.

"They don't hate you. That's not what I'm saying, Penelope. It's just that nobody is interested in buying this sort of thing right now," Liz said, her voice on the other end slow and patronizing, but mostly tired. Tired of me, in other words.

"Oh, bullshit!" I slammed the phone receiver into its base and stood up from my desk. Pacing back and forth, I couldn't stop my jaw from clenching and unclenching. *Bullshit is right! Not selling … when did I ever have a problem selling books?!*

Interest in true crime was at an all-time high. If it weren't for all those stupid armchair detectives and bloggers and TikTokers and Netflix ... perhaps people would still be interested in reading my hard-won research and "fiercely addictive tales", as the queen of crime herself once wrote in a blurb for me.

But that was then, and this was now. I hadn't sold a book in nearly a decade, and the book I wrote about the Terrehaute murders in the early 2000s was a big fat bust, barely earning back a quarter of the shockingly low advance they paid me.

"You're pacing again." My husband, Robert, entered my office, carrying two small cups of hot tea.

"Not now!" I said, waving him away. But Robert didn't listen to me—he never does—the only man to tolerate my brashness and misplaced anger.

He placed our teacups on the side table and came to me, pulling me in for a hug, even though he knew—after forty years of marriage—that I wasn't too fond of touching.

But somehow, leaning into his chest and smelling the comforting woodsy aroma of his aftershave, leveled out my breathing and brought me back down to earth. Getting angry would get me nowhere. I'd have to come up with something else to write about, offer a new package for my agent to sell ... something better. Bigger.

"I didn't mean to pry, but I heard bits and pieces," Robert said, softly. He released me from his arms and urged me over to the two cherry-red, leather reading chairs. The leather on the chairs was cracked and worn, just like us at age sixty-nine and seventy-three, and they were our favorite place to sit and chat, especially after a long day sitting at my desk, doing researching or punching keys on the keyboard.

"Then you know it didn't go well," I said, blowing steam from the top of my cup and venturing a small sip.

"Yes, I know. I'm sorry, Penn."

"Well, there's nothing to be sorry about. If they're not interested in the cult angle, then I'll have to look for something else. It's not like there's any shortage of crimes occurring in our country, these days…"

"Penn."

"What?" I took a long sip this time, waiting for him to say it. It wasn't the first time, or the last. He'd been trying to talk me off this ledge for the past twenty years.

"Why not retire, sweetheart? We don't need the money. You've already sold millions of copies of your books … you have nothing to prove anymore," he said.

I let out an angry laugh. "You of all people should know it's not about the money. It's about the work. The writing…"

"Yes, I know. But we aren't getting any younger, daffodil. I love that you still love to write. And I'm proud of all of your accomplishments. But I hate seeing you stressed out like this. I hate seeing the way they talk to you…"

By "they" he meant my agent and former publishers. I'd had many over the years—breaking things off for better opportunities or when they questioned my skills or tried to change too much of my work…

Yes, some might call me difficult. Okay, not some.

Anyone who collaborated with me between 1980 to 1995, knew that I was a literary diva and occasional hothead.

But I had to be! The literary world was so male dominated, especially then, and I had to make a name for myself. I wasn't Betty fucking Crocker, for god's sake, I was writing about some of the most gruesome and horrific crimes. They should have been prepared to deal with a woman with a backbone of steel!

"Let's take our walk, shall we?" Robert suggested. I held out my hand to Robert and he tugged me out of my chair. It used to seem romantic when he did that—holding me up and carrying me off to bed. But now I was getting old, and often, his touch and support were becoming more of a necessity, and less of a thrill.

"Yes, let's," I said, with a tight smile. He was patronizing me, just like my agent.

Everyone wanted me to throw in the towel, but I never would!

Moments later, we were leaving our massive eight-bedroom estate, and venturing into the swirling vines and flowers of the garden. I'd always loved the book, *The Secret Garden*, as a child. While I was gone on tour in 2002, Robert hired landscapers to build it for me.

Robert, despite his flaws and my career, had always been a godsend to me. He'd stood by my side, always supporting me—from the height of my career, and now down to its lowly bottom.

The sun was blaring, but the wind had a chill to it, the kind that seeps right through your skin and enters the bones. I shivered, clutching my shawl to my chest, just as Robert wrapped an arm around my shoulders and led me toward the garden he'd built for me. Robert was a wizard when it came to gardening.

My knees were stiff and achy these days, more than they'd ever been. Years of sitting at my desk had caused it, but my increasing years in age probably didn't help either.

"It's okay, my sweet daffodil. Nothing that the trees and flowers and the dirt can't fix," Robert said, his words like whispers in my hair beside me. He led me through the trellises and down a pebbled path, then we entered another world. A secret, enclosed garden of my very own—wrought iron furniture, a glittering koi pond full of fish, and rows and rows of flowers that stretched so far that I often lost sight of them.

"Oh, look at these. How they've grown since I saw them last," I murmured, reaching out to run my hands over the clusters of verbena, black-eyed Susans, mums, and nemesia. It was autumn now, but many of the flowers were late-bloomers, and we had a staff of gardeners to maintain them all year round.

"They're beautiful, just like you," Robert said, kissing the back of my hand and leading me to our favorite bench. It was made of limestone, and we had carved our initials in its seat many, many years ago. It felt like only yesterday, really.

"Sit. I need to show you something," he said.

I sat. Robert's announcement surprised me—it had been so long since he'd given me a gift or orchestrated something special for me. He knew I didn't like surprises, preferring to be involved—and often, in charge—of all our life decisions.

"Something came in the mail for you. I know I shouldn't have opened it, but you've been so stressed and busy ... and well, I'm sorry that I read it before you did," Robert said, sheepishly.

From his leather belt pouch, Robert withdrew a thick cream envelope, the seal already broken.

"Who's it from?" I said, taking it from his hand. Both of our parents and siblings were long gone, and Robert and I had never had children of our own. I didn't regret the fact that we didn't have kids, but I did miss having family, and other people to reach out to on the holidays. You might think I'd have lots of friends, made during my publishing career, but it wasn't so. The life of a writer is lonely, and mostly filled with business associates and critics, it seemed. I honestly had no idea who could have sent me a personal letter...

I slid the card out and let the envelope fall away.

Dear Penelope Jewel,

You are cordially invited to Beechwood Castle on November 9th, 2023, for a night you'll never forget...

I gasped. Then I looked up at Robert in anger.

"Why didn't you tell me about this right away? How long have you been holding onto this, Robert?"

Robert's face flushed crimson, his hands twisting the

envelope in his lap, the way he always did when he felt guilty.

"How long?" I demanded, scooting away from him. Of course, I'd heard the bizarre announcement—an anonymous new buyer of the old Beechwood Estate and the chance for six people to come in and check it out before renovations. I'd even mentioned it to Robert.

The whole thing brought up bad feelings for me ... when the massacre occurred, I'd had a strange feeling—a mixture of horror but also excitement too. All those years ago, I'd thought it would be me, authoring the story about what happened there. Who would be better to tell the tale than a renowned true crime writer who lived less than ten miles away from where the murders occurred?

But I was starting to struggle then, my old editors retiring and the new and up-and-comers looking at me with disdain. *Penelope Jewel, that old bat ... with her old-fashioned methods and stick-in-the-mud demands ... nobody wants to collaborate with her.* Nobody wanted to work with *me*.

And the Beechwood story went to someone else ... a hotshot, fresh-faced newbie, who secured a six-figure deal to write it. The book turned out terribly. Nobody remembers that part of the story, but I do.

I remember how I was passed over for a story that by every single right should have been mine!

But now I'll have another chance to write it. And from an insider's view!

"I've only had it for a few days," Robert finally said, a quiver in his voice. "You were so irritable and busy writing the proposal ... and I was kind of hoping we could get that RV like we talked about and hit the road before the holidays. I think you should retire, Penn ... and frankly, this Beechwood thing sounds potentially dangerous to me. Are you sure you're really up for it?"

I narrowed my eyes at my husband. He'd always been a coward, but rarely selfish.

"Stop patronizing me, Robert! Of course I'm going. No one could stop me, especially an annoying pissant like you."

Angrily, I yanked the wadded-up envelope out of his hand and stood, my legs wobbly beneath. Robert stood, trying to help me, but I shooed him away.

"I'm going inside to pack my things," I announced, leaving Robert where he sat in the garden he built for me. "And before you ask, I don't need any damn help from you," I shouted over my shoulder.

"Oh wait." I stopped, turned. "I need you to RSVP for me. That's the least you can do, eh?"

Chapter Five

Bonnie

I never liked the castle. Not even one little bit.

From the first moment I laid eyes on it until the last, I'd known it was a place filled with bad juju, and restless spirits—not the good kind of spirits, neither.

Most people don't recognize it—the unease in their stomachs, the tightness in their scalps, or the dizzying effects of the trees and forestry and rot-filled walls around them. But I knew in my heart of hearts—Beechwood Castle had always been evil.

When most people think about its history, they think about the Civil War. The Simon brothers reconstructed most of the original stone buildings, adding their own little flourishes to the property. But the Beechwood property was around long before that...

My great-grandmother and namesake, Bonnie, and her

mother before her, had deep ancestral roots in this town. 'Witches' people liked to call them. Although, now they call people like me 'psychics' if they're kind ... and 'charlatans' if they're disbelievers. Healers and dealers of the ancient art of spells and wizardry, my ancestors were more than a little familiar with the original Beechwood family of Rock Hill. An evil coven, practicing black magic, who performed satanic rituals and murdered anyone who trespassed there. At least that's what my mother and grandmother told me...

Before the post-Civil War era, the trees and the land itself were already cursed, with the blood of the innocents who were killed there. So, it came as no surprise to me that all these bad things happened in the nineties. It was only a matter of time...

The Simon brothers eventually killed their kids and wives; and then there were the fires that ran rampant, killing half the charges at the orphanage, and then of course —the most recent tragedy, those kids, butchered like pigs by an ax-wielding maniac.

As much as I tried not to think about the castle, I still dreamt of it often. I saw it how it was now, its crumbling walls and inner sanctums. A long dark tunnel leading outside. I often traveled there in my dreams, searching its halls for lost souls, and answers. At least that's what I'd like to believe...

But my psychic powers, though real, have remained inconsistent all of my life. Somewhere along the slippery slope of genetics, the powers of the Black family women had begun to fade. Unfortunately, I'd only been given a small touch of it, compared to those who came before in my family's lineage.

Which is how I got into all this trouble in the first place.

It started innocently enough; as a young woman, I traveled often, and alone, to places like the boardwalk in Atlantic City or the markets in New Orleans, offering palm reading, reading tarot cards, and interpreting tea leaves. I charged as little as one dollar for some and as much as a hundred dollars for others, depending on the clientele.

It wasn't good money; and, truth be told, I was terrible with the leaves and palmistry. But I made it work anyway.

Most people don't realize how much they give away about themselves, starting with the very first moment they meet you. From the clothes they wear, to whom they're with, to the way they carry themselves, or whether or not they're wearing an engagement ring... It's easy to figure out things about them and use canned readings to fit a general narrative that will appease them enough to leave them smiling on their way out, and hopefully pleased enough to leave an extra tip in my jar.

The money wasn't great—just enough to eat and sometimes enough to find a place to sleep for the night and put a little gas in the car. But then I met my husband, Marco, and everything changed after I became pregnant. With a hungry baby to feed and Marco's addiction to heroin even hungrier than the child, I had to find normal, suitable work. I tried; really, I did. Waiting tables, running cash registers, cleaning toilets ... I tried all of it. There was nothing I was "too good" for; I just wanted to keep my husband and child happy, and healthy.

But then I met a woman while working at a local pastry shop. She was sitting by herself at a tiny table, doing her own tarot cards. It was my ego that did it—"Let me do that for you. It's better if someone else reads them to you, even if you're an expert yourself," I told her, solemnly.

So, the woman let me read her tarot cards and from there, it started—a friendly, but mostly business-like relationship—with the woman who called herself Raquel Cashmere. Raquel was an esteemed "psychic to the stars" and "whisperer to the dead". She ran an online telephone business, and she also traveled to people's homes to offer her services. Eventually, she brought me in as her assistant.

I admired Raquel—not for her psychic abilities (they were shit), but for the cunning way she drew a crowd, and the way she always made money. It all seemed innocent enough at first—charge them by the minute to talk and predict their futures, charge them to cleanse their houses, talk to their dead spouses and children, provide them with love potions and bogus spells. It was clear that Raquel was married to making money, not the art of divination.

I thought I was doing good work for a while, but when she started stealing credit card numbers and taking advantage of the elderly and grieving families, I should have broken away from her right then. But the money was too good; sure, Marco was snorting or shooting half of it, but I still cleared enough to buy a cute house in the suburbs of Rock Hill, where I'd been born and raised, and enough to put food on the table, diapers on the baby, and clothes on our backs. That felt like luxury to me.

But then the investigation happened. And when it did, Raquel skipped town, leaving me with a bomb in my hands —all of her phony LLCs registered in my name, most of her fraudulent transactions tracked back to me, in one way or another. And when the police arrived at the house to arrest me, my sweet baby was barely out of diapers and Marco had left me in a house with a kilo of heroin that didn't belong to me.

So, that's how I wound up in federal prison. I served ten years, and I deserved all ten of them.

All of those "blessings" handed down to me by my ancestors had caused me nothing but pain. I never read another palm or did any tarot in prison, but I did spend a lot of time in my own head, focusing on astral projection, predictions, and mind control while I rotted in that dirty cell.

Though mostly useless, my abilities did keep me from going insane while I was in there.

I'd been out for seven years now, living the straight-and-narrow life with my sister Sue, back at my old house in Rock Hill, working a job my parole officer helped me get at the JayC's food store. Mostly, I'd been trying to forget about my life from before.

My daughter Cecilia was taken away by the state after I was convicted. Marco died while I was in prison, OD. After losing my daughter, losing him felt like nothing—like a minor hiccup after suffering cardiac arrest…

Day in and day out, my life was boring. I still read mine and my sister's palms; I still had occasional visions that were blurry and confusing, at best. But then I saw the news headlines ... the reopening of Beechwood Castle. The mysterious new owner and the random six invitees...

There was never a doubt in my mind—I knew I would be selected as one of the six.

The dreams began right after I read about it in the paper; dreams that involved me, wandering through those old corridors, graffiti walls and blood splattered concrete floors ... almost like a ghost anchored to the ceiling, I could see myself inside the castle. I could see myself, searching for its secrets and lies. *But why?*

I don't know what my purpose at Beechwood Castle will be, but I was always destined to be chosen.

At least, that's what the spirits told me. But the rational side of me—the one who did her time and lost it all because of those abilities—was feeling doubtful.

So, when the invitation arrived in the mail, I wasn't surprised, but I also wasn't relieved. I felt validation, knowing what I used to believe before my sentence—that my psychic abilities were real, and that they would serve some sort of purpose in the future—was actually true. But I couldn't shake off this gnawing feeling, that something really bad would happen if I went there.

The thirty-six pages of waivers and NDAs that arrived only days after I accepted the invitation ... I did not predict those.

My sister Sue sat at our kitchen table, drinking gin and

smoking a Marlboro, flipping through the documents, page by page.

"This is nuts, Bonnie. You do know that, right?" She flicked a page, a pillowy cloud of ashes falling to the floor.

"It doesn't matter what those papers say." I huffed, pouring a glass of tea and digging through our cupboards for sweetener. *If the fates want me there, then I'm going. The worst things in life have already happened to me ... what more can I expect? Nothing I can't manage.*

"What about your parole officer, huh? You're not allowed to go anywhere overnight, unless you get it approved by her," Sue reminded me. I didn't need any reminders. I followed my parole guidelines to the T, never wanting to return to that box again...

But my sister was right, of course. It was nuts. There were only four months left of my parole. It was an unnecessary risk.

However, I was a model parolee, paying all my fees and staying out of trouble. I suspected that my parole officer would probably say okay if I asked, but I wasn't taking any chances that she might refuse.

"If she finds out, I'll just ask for forgiveness later," I said, sliding into the seat across from my sister. "Now, let me see those papers again."

Sue wasn't a lawyer, but she was smart. She did the bookkeeping for a local garbage and sanitation company, and she was always the wisest of the two of us—having eight years on me.

I knew I should have felt grateful toward her; after all,

she swooped in and saved the house from foreclosure, and she helped me get back on my feet after prison. But I would never forgive her for what she didn't save—my daughter. I would have let the house turn to rubble and my body to dust, before letting Cecilia get carted off to foster care. But Sue never was much of a kid person. And we never talked about Cecilia, even when I tried to bring her up. The one time Sue talked about her, it was to say: "She's probably better off, Bonnie." In that moment, I'd wanted to slap her face harder than I'd ever wanted to slap anyone's, including those social workers who took her away and the pompous judge who sentenced me.

"It's a lot. But it's standard, in some cases. Especially for people who go on TV shows," Sue was talking, pointing at the papers in my hand. "Is that what you think this is, Bonnie? Reality TV or some kind of documentary they're doing about the murders?"

I shrugged, trying to look at the pages in front of me, but they were all just a blur. I was going to sign them regardless.

"I don't think it's a documentary. If it is, it makes no sense to have me there. I hung out at the castle when I was a kid. Most kids around here did back then … but I wasn't there when the murders happened. And I barely knew those kids who died."

"I never hung out there," Sue said, stubbing out her cigarette and reaching for another.

"Well, you were always the smart one, remember?" I flashed a half-smile and she laughed at that. Moments like these, I truly loved her. I had to—she was the only family I had left in this world.

"It could be some sort of ghost show. They want us to wander around so they can take video footage of us. Or maybe they just want to use us as bait, in case there is something demonic there."

Sue chuckled at that, but I didn't. That place had always given me an eerie feeling, even back when we were kids. Sue was blessed by not having the sight of our mother; and she had always considered my abilities to be "hogwash".

"It's an NDA and medical waivers. An agreement not to bring in any unapproved items, including camera equipment. That includes your phone too, Bonnie … it's just a lot. All of this worries me," Sue said, her face turning serious now.

"It worries me too," I said, surprised by my own honesty. "But I'm going anyway, Sis. I have a feeling I'm meant to be there."

Sue released a deep sigh as I lifted my pen. Without reading the rest, I moved from page to page, scribbling my signature on the dotted lines.

Chapter Six

Rad

"Coffee, black. And some of that leftover pumpkin pie, with whipped cream, please." I handed the sticky plastic menu to the young, brunette waitress with the thick, drawn-on brows, and offered her a tight smile. She was new here at Joey's Diner, which meant she didn't know me well enough to hate me yet. Most of the people in this town, my age or older, knew enough to keep their distance from me.

To be honest, somedays I wish I could get some distance from me too.

"Sure thing, mister." She had a kind smile; oh, how I'd forgotten what it felt like to be liked, or respected.

She was back within minutes with my coffee and pie. The crust was too hard and the coffee too cold, but I downed them anyway while I waited.

When the door to the diner opened and I heard a bell

chime, I didn't have to look to know it was Jimmy. Jimmy Duplantis, my longtime lawyer and lifelong friend. Well, "lifelong" if friends since teenage-hood were the same thing.

Jimmy slid into the booth right next to me with a heavy sigh.

"Jesus, Jimmy. It's not like we're on a date," I said, scooting as close to the window and away from him as possible. He'd gained nearly fifty pounds since his retirement, and he still sweated like a pig, even in autumn.

"Well, we need some privacy for this, Rad," he said, sliding a manilla file folder toward me and signaling for the waitress to come. After he'd ordered a stack of pancakes and a glass of milk, we got down to business.

"So, what do you think?" I said, shuffling the packs of sweeteners on the table. The folder was still set in front of me, unopened. I didn't need to see the documents; I'd already read them a dozen times before handing them over to Jimmy to peruse.

"What do I think?" Jimmy took a long swig of his coffee then pushed the cup and saucer aside. "I think you'd be a damn fool to sign these, that's what. No one in their right mind would do this."

"Good thing my mind is already fucked," I growled, running my hands through my thinning brown hair. I, too, had gained weight since my retirement. And I was looking just as shabby and worn-down as Jimmy these days. Two old boys, that's all we were. We used to be the cool kids—

sporty and strong, with a gaggle of friends and girls to choose from when it came to filling our time.

He chose law school, and I chose what I was always meant to do—what my father and my granddaddy and half my uncles and cousins did—law enforcement. I can't remember a time in which I didn't want to be a cop. I just always knew I would be one.

My career high was short-lived and devastating; the only solace was that my father didn't live long enough to see my demise.

"You're basically signing away all your rights, Rad. By signing these papers, you're agreeing not to sue them if you get injured or killed. You're also giving up any and all rights to privacy. They can film you and edit that film to look like whatever they want. And you can't say anything about your experience until it's over. Even then, you have to be debriefed on what you can say. I'd love to know who in the hell came up with this plan. The signature on the documents is just for 'Beechwood LLC', and frankly, my friend, that's shady as fuck."

"I know, and that's exactly why I have to go there. Can I tell you something, Jimmy? Even if I hadn't received an invitation to the castle, I probably would have found a way to sneak inside. Someone in this town is up to something, I just don't know what it is," I said, tapping on the folder. I was talking too loudly—I always did that—and the new, hot waitress was watching us from the corner of her eye behind the counter, I could feel it.

I lowered my voice, "I need to know what this

anonymous new buyer has planned at the castle. Why now, after all these years? It's important to find out what's going on…"

"I don't think I need to remind you, old friend, but you're not police anymore," Jimmy said.

"I haven't been police for a long time. The moment I screwed up that case and killed that kid, my career as a cop was over. They might have let me keep my badge and I stayed out of jail, thanks to you, but I've never felt the same since. No other interesting cases ever crossed my desk, and half the people in this town won't look at me, not after they think I murdered the suspected killer of those kids back then."

Jimmy rested a hand on my shoulder. "Is there any point in wasting my breath here, Rad? It sounds like your mind is already made up."

I nodded. "You're right. It was made up the moment I heard about it on the news. But I do appreciate you looking over these documents. If shit goes sideways at this event, I might need your help getting me out of trouble again. Who knows, Jimmy? Maybe you'll get to come bail me out of jail again, after all these years."

I grinned at my friend, but he didn't smile back. His face was stone cold serious.

"If you're doing this, promise me you'll be careful. It could be something stupid—some nutjob who wants to make a documentary and catch you off guard with questions about those murders and about the Reeks kid. You should be prepared for that. But it's not only that … it could be something more sinister. There's a lot of sickos in this world, Rad. You know that better than anybody," Jimmy said.

"I do." Bobby Reeks. I'd spent the last couple decades trying to forget him … but then I heard that announcement over the radio.

Yes, I killed him. But I didn't do it on purpose.

Reeks was the prime suspect in the castle murders right from the get-go. His family owned adjacent property to those woods and Reeks was known to run around in them, messing with kids he didn't like in the woods and prodding at animals with a stick. We even found his semen near the crime scene; he'd been jerking off in those woods, apparently obsessed with one of the girls from the group that died. One of the girls had spotted him earlier in the night and when I went to confront him … well, the rest is local history. He ran through those woods like a bat out of hell, jumping logs and zigzagging between trees. I was twenty-five then, fresh out of the academy, hot-headed as hell, and my adrenaline thumping—not with fear, like it should have been, but pure, unadulterated glee. My first big arrest, and it would be a mass murderer. I'd imagined my name in the headlines, a big promotion… Perhaps a huge job in the city, solving real crimes and taking out the worst of the worst in our society.

But that's not what happened to me. I shot the kid, our only suspect. But I didn't mean to shoot him. The gun went off by accident. I was fresh out of training, and I'd been so eager to go confront him and chase him down that I'd forgotten to turn the safety on.

I took out my piece, shouted for him to freeze, and then the fucking thing just went off.

The kid didn't know what hit him. But I knew—a nine-millimeter cartridge to the back. It ricocheted around his spinal column before striking his heart.

I panicked, of course. There was this seemingly rational voice in my head, telling me that no one was around to see it. *I took out the killer. Maybe I'll say he attacked me, and I fought back valiantly. A hero who solved the case and killed the monster dead on his feet.*

But when I went to the kid and saw the gaping red wound, I found the reason he was running. A dime bag of pot fell from his hand. A few mushrooms in his pocket. Turns out, Reeks was a low-level drug dealer, digging up mushrooms in the woods, planting some crappy marijuana, and scaring off other kids who came around because he didn't want his stash uncovered.

Afterwards, when they searched his parents' place, they found no murder weapon. No blood. And the shoeprints we found at the crime scene didn't match any shoes inside Reeks's parents' house.

Basically, I'd killed a drug dealer who had little or no real connection to the murder. He was just a fucking kid.

Of course, plenty of the locals still thought he did it. They thought I'd blown it—those murdered kids' parents never got answers, or a true sense of justice. Most days I liked that theory. Because the alternative was much worse—

that the real killer got away with those murders and could still be walking among the townspeople of Rock Hill...

It seemed unlikely that the killer was still around, if it wasn't Bobby Reeks that did it. But still... For years, I'd waited for something to happen—a murder or something to bring me back to that case. But nothing did. It was all traffic stops, domestics, and minor drug busts from then on out. And no one in my department liked me.

I finished my second cup of coffee and paid for both of us. "I appreciate you coming Jimmy, and for looking over the papers. But, like you said, my mind's already made up."

Jimmy followed me out of the diner, his back bent and his knees cracking, and he wasn't much worse for wear than I was.

"Well, good luck old friend. It's been a pleasure," Jimmy said.

We shook hands and said our goodbyes, as though I were headed off to war—or hell—instead of just some stupid overnight prank night in the middle of the woods.

I wanted to laugh about it—my stubbornness, Jimmy's nagging ... but I couldn't. I couldn't shake off the feeling that Jimmy was right. That something sinister was being planned, perhaps specifically as a punishment for me. For what I did to that kid in the woods, and for letting those murdered children and their families down all those years ago.

~rsvp~

You might be tempted to pause, to freeze the frame. To study each player, one by one, like intricate pieces of a jigsaw puzzle.

But the more you look, the more out of focus they'll become ... because none of their motives for coming to the castle are clear.

You might call them outcasts.

Some might consider them traitors.

They aren't known for making (or keeping) friends.

Certainly not the psychic fraudster, the snobby writer, or Staci Stretch-the-Truth Adams. And we can't forget about our resident Peeping Tom—no one will be rooting for him, that's for sure.

But the cop and the girl ... they are two sides of the same coin. One cowered from danger and saved her life, while the other charged at it like a crazy bull and ruined his and many others.

So, how will they handle the scent of danger this time—fight or flight?

Soon, we will find out.

Tick tock.

Chapter Seven

~SIX O'CLOCK~

The Hostess

One by one, I watched them arrive. Like lambs to the slaughter, I thought, grimly.

Promptly, I shook away that negative thought and put a smile on my face.

"Hello there! You must be Penelope Jewel. Please head inside and take one of the seats in the front room. I'll be with you shortly, when the rest of our guests arrive."

The aging author opened her mouth as though it were full of bees, but I held up a hand in protest. "Please hold all questions until the others arrive," I said, polite but firm.

The disgruntled and entitled author swished past me and entered the castle. The heavy front doors were wedged open behind me, and I could hear Penelope in there, questioning the catering staff as they wheeled out long silver platters for the guests' dinner. Carefully, I listened for a response but there was none.

Good, I thought, smugly. Like me, the caterers had been instructed not to ask questions and most importantly, not to answer any. Unless they were questions we'd been instructed to answer.

Resuming my post at the front door, I watched the rest of our guests arrive. First, it had been the author. Then the ex-cop. Then the psychic, the architect, and the YouTuber. Last but not least, the victim, or so-called 'final-girl' of the massacre that took place here years ago.

I pretended not to know anything about them, besides their names. As I'd been instructed to do.

Each guest had been transported individually, driven here by paid Uber and Lyft drivers, and brought right to the front gates of Beechwood.

It was a long drive in—I'd suffered the drive myself in my own Uber hours earlier—a windy and gravelly ascent, the woods growing thicker the closer I came to the property, forming a tunnel of trees all around me. Spooky vibes. Despite the sunlight and the crisp autumn air, there was no denying those vibes...

The castle itself and the main expanse of the property were sealed off from the world by heavy wrought iron gates and surrounded with electric wire. Any small gaps in the iron fencing were reinforced with electric fencing and chicken wire. As it was explained to me, this was done to keep out young children, reckless teens, and careless adults when the property was abandoned in the mid-seventies.

Later, the security would serve a different purpose—to keep out nosy reporters, twisted true crime freaks, and those with more sinister purposes after the massacre.

But today, those gates were wide open for our guests. Each guest was met on the other side by two armed guards who checked for weapons and contraband—for the guests' own safety, of course. Their small backpacks and suitcases were sifted through, to make sure they had followed the rules. All of them.

Those rules included—no cameras. No cell phones. No recording devices of any kind. No weapons. No food or drinks. No alcohol or drugs. Nothing besides approved medications, essential clothing, toiletries, and a small list of approved personal items.

The guests were aware of the risks—supposedly. Like me, they had signed a lengthy contract, agreeing to be filmed and recorded, while also agreeing not to do the same in return. They had signed medical waivers in case of injury —these old structures were built to last, but you never know. And they had agreed to forfeit the money if they didn't follow the rules, or if they left the site, of their own accord or by someone else's.

Personally, I thought they were all bananas for coming. But it wasn't my place to judge. I had a job to do, and I planned to do it well. My time here was limited, and it came with its own hefty paycheck.

One by one, I greeted the guests as they moved through the security checkpoint and entered the walls of the castle. It wasn't a real castle by anyone's standards—just an old structure in the woods, in my opinion. Frankly, the whole place made me feel like an extra on the set of *The Walking Dead*, or some other dystopian TV show in which the world has been abandoned, everybody left for dead…

When all of the guests had entered and the gates were resealed and the guards were relieved, I tugged the heavy timber doors closed behind me and latched the metal bolt to keep us in.

All eyes were on me as I entered the foyer and took to the center of the floor. The psychic, the architect, and the YouTuber were squeezed together on a dusty velvet longue; the author was sitting in a heavy, wing-backed blue chair and looked mildly disgusted as she attempted to dust off her trousers; the ex-cop was trying to find a seat by the final girl, but she practically growled at him, refusing to move an inch on the tattered beige sofa she had chosen. Eventually, the ex-cop decided to stand, with his back to the wall by the fireplace, and his arms crossed over his chest. He looked uneasy, but so did the rest of them.

"Welcome, guests." I clasped my hands in front of me like I'd practiced, trying to look as serious—yet polite—as possible, per my instructions. I didn't bring note cards with me—at least not inside the castle—but I didn't need them anyway. The words were rehearsed in my head.

"I know each of you has many questions. But first, please allow me to introduce myself." I cleared my throat and offered a small smile that went unreturned. Each guest was looking around them, some mesmerized and others in horror, at the rotten planks on the floor and the walls made of solid stone and rubble. The castle felt less like a structure, and more like an ancient tomb, hidden away in the forest … reserved for scary bedtime stories.

"My name is Mary Beth Penner. And before I go any further, let me say … I am not the one who brought you here."

"Wait … what?" Staci, the young YouTuber, said, scooting closer to the edge of the longue. Her viewers on YouTube called her 'Stabby Staci', which implied tough vibes, if you asked me … but I couldn't see it. She was a tiny wisp of a thing, with half-moons under her eyes and a sprinkle of acne on her chin. She looked like a stiff breeze could knock her over, or that a minor wrong detail might ruin her day…

I held up my hand again, grateful I'd gotten a manicure this week.

"Please hold all questions until the end. Like I said, I'm Miss Penner. I've been hired to host parts of this event. You have already seen the caterers coming and going. Please, pay them no mind. They are merely setting up for your dinner and they will be leaving the premises right after."

I took a breath, hoping that the menu I'd planned would be followed to the T. I wasn't familiar with the caterers; we'd had only a brief introduction before setting up. But they seemed capable, and the food looked like the menu I'd asked for.

"Anyways, I do not know why each of you are here, nor who arranged this event. My only function is to give you instructions and to make sure your dinner is served promptly at six-fifteen. That's in twelve minutes," I said, glancing at my watch, anxiously. "Nightly libations and snacks will be served this evening at ten o'clock. If you get hungry or thirsty in between those times, the kitchen is stocked with water, tea, soda, and some small dry-good snacks."

"Where are the cameras?" Lolly, our poor sweet final girl, asked. Internally, I sighed. But I gave the girl a pleasant smile anyway—I'd been specifically instructed to go easy on her, considering she was the victim of that horrendous massacre in 1996. "I'm sorry, but I know nothing about the placement of cameras," I told her.

Which was true. I didn't.

I followed the guests' gazes as they each turned around in their seats and looked around the dark foyer. It was a cold and dank room, with very little lighting from the stone-cut windows. Massive stone fireplaces lined each side of the room, the hearths taller than my own head. Neither were lit, and thankfully, I hadn't received any instructions about making fires.

"Cameras are so small these days. Have you seen those pinhole cameras or cameras that look like plants or lightbulbs? It doesn't take much to hide a camera," Cornelius, the perverted architect, said.

"You would know," said Bonnie, our resident psychic, scooting as far away from him on the longue as possible.

I bit back a smile. A few of them obviously were already acquainted with one another. "Guests, please. Allow me to finish my instructions, so that I can send you all to the dining hall for dinner. The sooner we get this done, the sooner each of you will be to collecting your share of a million dollars."

Now, finally, all eyes were turned on me.

"As I said, dinner is at six-fifteen and nightcaps are at ten. Each guest is required to participate in these gatherings. That is part of the rules. At the end of dinner, you will find one or more sealed envelopes in the center of the table. You all may take turns reading or designate one of you to read the instructions. These are coming from your main host, who has chosen to remain anonymous at this time. All bedrooms can be found on the second floor. Each room has your individual name on a placard on the door, so it will be clear whose room is whose. You may leave your belongings here in the foyer, until dinner has concluded. After dinner, you all may collect your belongings and retreat to your rooms if you desire. And if there are further instructions from your main host on the cards you receive after dinner, then there may be additional obligations, or tasks, for you to perform. I'm unsure about that. My function here is to greet you and make sure you all are well-fed and well-watered during your brief stay at the castle." I drew in a breath, my own throat parched from the robotic speech I'd memorized.

"Which room will you be staying in?" asked Staci, adjusting her bouncy black ponytail. It was tied up with one of those awful, poufy scrunchies that all the girls wore in the nineties, and with the acne on her face, she looked like the youngest of the bunch, barely twenty-five.

"I will not be staying in the castle, and neither will the

caterers. Once dinner is served, the caterers will leave through the gates and not return."

"And you?" Staci pressed.

"I will be staying in the small guest cottage across the way," I explained, pointing back at the heavy wooden doors we'd come through.

"But what if there's an emergency?" Lolly asked. Of everyone, she looked the most uncomfortable, picking at her nails. I'd also noticed she kept glancing angrily at Rad, the ex-cop. He also looked uncomfortable in her presence. I got the feeling these guests knew each other better than my employer had let on in his written instructions, at least some of them. But that wasn't my business, or my concern.

"Yes, let's talk about emergencies, shall we? As each of you know from the documents you received, cell phones are not permitted on the premises. However, there are two guarded men at the gates, and they can help out if there's an emergency. There should be no need for that, but you never know."

"And what if we decide we want out?" Bonnie asked, watching me intensely. Earlier, she'd looked like a big bag of nerves. But now, she looked positively focused—specifically on me. I'd never cared much for psychics or healers, and I didn't believe in all that mumbo jumbo. But Bonnie's gaze washing over me filled me with unease, as though she were undressing me with her eyes, removing my clothes and peeling back layers of skin...

I shook my head at myself and re-clasped my hands, trying not to show my annoyance. "Per the instructions each of you received ... you may leave the estate at any time. And as per your instructions, which I'm sure each of you read carefully before you came, the choice to come, and to go, is yours, and yours alone. If you leave, obviously, you will be forfeiting your share of the prize money."

"When will we get the money?" Cornelius asked. He was standing now, and he'd wandered over to inspect the wall next to one of the fireplaces. He ran his hand over its cold, bumpy surface, then made a face.

This time, I couldn't contain the sigh. According to my watch, dinner was only a few minutes away...

"Please refer to your paperwork for that. I'm not equipped with all the answers, but I do believe that the funds will be distributed to all of your bank accounts within three business days after leaving the castle," I said.

I was about to dismiss them for dinner, when I thought of one more thing.

"Ah! I almost forgot. Electricity. It works. Obviously," I said, pointing at the glowing yellow bulbs in the old-fashioned chandelier above our heads. While the house was rundown and still held remnants of its past, it was clear to me that my employer had added new touches—the chandelier that looked ancient, but really wasn't. The musty furniture that he (or she) probably picked up from Goodwill...

"However, these old structures are strange, and the electricity can be faulty at times, according to my employer. If you lose electricity, that does not mean you may leave. Unless you want to forfeit, of course. There are candles, matches, and flashlights in the kitchen drawers. Please do not take any candles upstairs to your individual rooms, for safety reasons. Also, the third-floor access to the tower has been sealed off due to safety concerns. So, please do not attempt to explore that area. That's part of the rules. Any other questions?"

"Many," Rad, the ex-cop said, speaking up for the first time. His mouth was held in a grim line; he didn't look nervous, exactly, just weary.

"Well then. I will escort you to the dining hall for dinner," I said, primly.

As I led our six guests through a dark corridor, following the clank of platters and utensils by the staff, I felt a rush of relief. Not only because dinner was starting right on time, but because I couldn't wait to get the hell away from this cursed place.

Chapter Eight

~SIX THIRTY O'CLOCK~

Staci

S ix of us sitting in a circle in the dark. The only thing between us was the knotty pine table and the silence that stretched and expanded the room, filling me with a sense of anxiety, but also excitement.

I'd never been known as chatty; hell, during my depressive episodes, I'd sometimes go days without speaking to my brother, sister-in-law, or friends. *But there's something about being here that gives me a new sense of confidence. I'm here for my viewers. I'm here to find out the truth. And I don't know any of these people, so who cares?*

"Well, if no one else is going to speak up, then I'll go first," I said, stabbing a fancy-looking, herb-infused potato with my fork.

There was something sinister about this place, but I kind

of liked it. The earthy, dank smell of it—the dark corridors, almost tomb-like.

Always drawn to the macabre, I found myself more intrigued than ever about this creepy stone palace in the woods. It had a history—I knew that—but like most versions of history and local legend, it had been rewritten and retold by the people with the power to tell things. A group of women living in the forest—a "coven of witches", as local legend goes—were finally driven out by the locals who considered their strange and eccentric behavior to be "blasphemous" and evidence of "witchcraft".

They were tortured and burned, supposedly. And as legend goes, all of those who came after the Beechwoods— the owners of the orphanage, the soldier siblings after the Civil War ... all were met with bad endings and fates, courtesy of the dark souls of the witches inside it.

But throughout my short career, researching cases of missing and murdered women, I'd long since learned that most monsters are humans; that witches were actually women who suffered, not storybook hags with brooms and warts; and that the only real thing to fear in life when it comes to violence is the evil indifference of my fellow species.

The long drive into the property had been otherworldly and breathtaking—gnarly, twisted trees and boggy patches of land; and the property itself looked like the former set of a fairytale movie, long since abandoned, with its broken, stone fountains, cherubs, and birdbaths. I didn't have a good grasp on the interior yet, but as Mary Beth Penner (*who the hell is she?* I wondered again) escorted us to the dining hall, I realized that the castle was a maze of dark corridors and dank rooms. I couldn't wait to explore it further.

And the dining hall itself was massive, big enough to fit several rooms inside it. The walls and ceiling looked broken, wet cracks forming in the stone, fuzzy bits of moss coming through, as though the forest itself was determined to consume it. The windows I'd seen so far were few, and all located higher than normal windows, making it hard to see outside, and limiting the amount of sunlight seeping in. Some of the windows in the dining hall were covered in thick, steel bars.

Clearing my throat, I tried again: "I'll start. My name is Staci. I go by 'Stabby Staci' online. That's my YouTube name... I run a channel called 'The Forgotten and the Lost' with—well, I run it by myself now. I have no idea why I was selected to come here, but I'm interested to get to know all of you and find out more about this place."

The man sitting to my right, whose large elbows and knees kept knocking into mine, pushed back his platter of food and sat up straight.

"Well, I'll go next then. I'm Cornelius Jones. I have a degree in architecture. I'm assuming that's why I was chosen to come," he said, proudly, sitting up straight in his chair.

The old woman sitting across from me, with the pantsuit and thousand-dollar diamond earrings, snorted and gave Cornelius a funny look.

"I know who both of you are," she said, mysteriously, cocking one of her tattooed eyebrows at me. She had barely touched her pork roast, carrots, and potatoes, turning up her nose at the food—and all of us too, from the moment she came through the front doors.

"Oh?" I said, leaning in so I could catch every word from across the table. She looked old and rich, not the sort of company I usually kept.

"That's right," the woman said with a smug nod and grin. She pointed a potato at me. "You're that armchair detective who makes up lies and then reports on them to get views. And you," she said, shifting her gaze to Cornelius, "you're the pervert who was peeping in women's windows last fall. You got arrested at the Dollar General. Or was it JayC's? I don't recall that detail."

"Hey, that was a misunderstanding…" Cornelius protested. He shrank in his seat, his face and neck turning crimson.

"Which part of it was misunderstood? The peeping in windows, your pants around your ankles, or the cock you were stroking in your hand?"

I nearly choked, trying not to laugh as I took a sip of water from my fancy goblet. I didn't like being called out for the lies on my channel, but I was sort of enjoying the horrified look on Cornelius's face. If he really was a pervert, then he probably deserved it. And this would be an interesting thing to talk about on my channel…

"Okay, you have my attention. Who are you, then?" I said, matching the smirk on her face with mine.

"Oh, honey. Any true crime reporter worth her salt would know who I am," she sniffed. "So what does that say about you and your little YouTube channel, huh? My name is Penelope Jewel and my true crime novels have sold over six million copies and been translated into a dozen languages around the world."

My eyes widened in surprise. Of course I knew of Penelope Jewel's work in the eighties and nineties; I simply hadn't recognized her face. And in my defense, her face was much older than the author photo she'd been using in her books.

"Congratulations on your success, Ms. Jewel," the overweight man beside Penelope interrupted. He had been super quiet from the get-go, hanging around the fringes of the group when we gathered in the foyer. Unlike the others, he did look vaguely familiar to me. Something about those hooded, haunting eyes…

"I'm Rad and I'm retired. Nice to meet all of you," he said quickly, mixing a hunk of meat with a potato and shoving it all in his mouth. I got the sense that he didn't want to be here at all, but I was still too focused on Penelope Jewel and the fact that another true crime person had been invited. Cornelius, the pervert, bumped his elbow with mine again. I scooted my chair over an inch to get away from him.

"Retired from what, exactly?" came another voice from the end of the table. This time it was the woman with the pale green eyes. She didn't look old—maybe forties—but there was a weariness to her face, thick wrinkles and crow's feet on her forehead and around her strange, sad eyes.

"You know what I'm retired from, Lolly. And it's good to see you again, by the way," Rad said, glancing down the table at her.

"It's not good to see you," the woman named Lolly muttered, pushing back from her plate.

"Wait," I said, examining the woman closer. There was something familiar in those sad, pale eyes... "Are you Lolly Andrews?" I said, kicking myself for not seeing the resemblance earlier. The girl who survived the Beechwood Massacre was young and blonde, with bold eyes and a pretty smile, based on her old school photographs. But the woman sitting here now was a darker version, a tired and devastated and washed-out ghost of her former self.

"Yes," Lolly said simply, still staring at Rad.

"The true crime expert scores another point!" jeered Penelope, smirking at me from across the table.

"I can't believe they invited you here, Lolly. Well, I can. But I just can't believe you came. Isn't this hard for you? It must be difficult, being back in this place where your friends ... well, you know..." I said, excitement building in my chest like a bomb. I knew this feeling, this growing excitement and proclivity for conversation—I was on the verge of a manic episode.

Lolly gave me a long, hard look.

The overweight man named Rad coughed. "Can we not question Lolly right now? Let's finish our food in peace. We just have to get through the night and then we can all get the hell out of here," he said, briskly.

"You never answered the question, though," Cornelius said, pointing his fork at Rad with a deep frown on his face. The blush of embarrassment from earlier was gone; he looked almost angry now.

"Most of you probably already know what I'm retired from, that's why. I retired from the police force," Rad said.

"That's one way of putting it," said Lolly, darkly. Finally, she picked up a baby carrot and popped it in her mouth.

That's when it hit me—how could I be so blind? This man was Rad Williams, the cop who bungled the case and killed Bobby Reeks, the prime suspect in the massacre all those years ago. He was hated afterwards for it, the townspeople blaming him for their lack of justice for those poor, dead kids…

"Do you still live in Rock Hill, Rad?" I asked.

Rad nodded, and gave me a long look, his first time really meeting me eye to eye. He had the heavy gaze of a detective, evaluating me.

"I'm surprised you stayed around here," I said, softly. "Wait. Are we all from Rock Hill? I figured that most of the invitees would be from different parts of the country…"

I looked from face to face, evaluating my temporary roommates, as they each nodded and confirmed my suspicions.

"How strange," I said, thoughtfully. *Who would bring us here? And for what reason? Why did they choose us specifically, and only local residents of Rock Hill?* A tug of fear was growing inside me. The fact that we were all here, residents of Rock Hill and some of us with connections to the tragedy and true crime, couldn't be an accident. We were chosen, the selection process not random at all, apparently…

And from what I could see so far, there was no evidence of cameras—small or large—and no recording devices in place. If this were for a TV show, we all would have been fitted with mics … right?

What role do I play in all of this, whatever this is? I wondered, the wheels turning ceaselessly in my brain.

The woman at the end of the table, in her bright blue shawl and turquoise, dangly earrings, cleared her throat. She'd spoken earlier in the foyer, but she'd been quiet ever since taking her seat at the table, choosing to watch us instead of participating. She, too, looked strangely familiar to me, but I couldn't figure out why. In her forties or fifties, she looked older with her attire—the eccentric jewels and the layered shawls. The grandmotherly dress she was wearing…

"I guess I'm last to go. I'm Bonnie Black," she said. "I also live in Rock Hill. And before anyone calls me out for my misdeeds, I'll go ahead and tell you that I served time in prison on fraud and drug charges years ago. I have no connection to the massacre that happened here. I'm not a true crime guru or a detective. So, I have no clue why I've been brought here. But here I am…" Patiently, I waited for more, but Bonnie didn't give it. There was something else she was holding back from us; but, if she was willing to tell us about her criminal past, then why not tell it all?

Perhaps my spidey senses were off when it came to Bonnie. But I could feel a buzzing in my brain, trying to unravel the reasons we had all been brought here.

I looked, again, from face to face, taking them all in. Not such a strange combination of people when you considered where we were—Lolly was a victim of the massacre and Rad was one of the policemen involved in the original investigation. Penelope and I were true crime buffs, and the perv next to me was an architect, so maybe they just invited him along because of that credential. But the lady at the end —Bonnie—I wasn't sure what she was doing here yet, or why her face looked a little familiar now that I was staring at it.

I couldn't wait to find out more about my fellow invitees, so I could report back to my viewers.

"Can you point me in the direction of the bathroom?" I asked, trying to catch Lolly's eye from across the table. She'd gone earlier, before joining us at the table for dinner.

"It's through the kitchen, and down the hall," Lolly said, flatly, pointing.

"Thank you." I'd barely touched my food, but I stood and made my way toward the swinging doors of the kitchen.

When I walked inside, I found it full of catering staff in thick white aprons. They were packing up and preparing to leave. They had served our food and then made themselves sparse as soon as we sat down for dinner; so much so, that I'd nearly forgotten we weren't alone here in the castle.

Mary Beth Penner was standing at the kitchen stove, speaking quietly with one of the workers.

"Looking for the restroom?" she said, smiling politely at me.

I nodded.

Stiffly, she led me through another door in the kitchen down a short, dark hallway. It was lined with photographs, and I reminded myself that I would need to look those over later when I got the chance to explore.

"It's to your right," Mary Beth said, nodding down the long dark hallway.

"Thank you."

I slipped inside the tiny washroom, locking the door behind me and flipping a switch on the wall. The yellow bulb over the sink buzzed noisily. I'd expected the bathroom facilities to be decent, but the sink looked like a basin for washing farm animals, and the toilet was old and stained, like someone had tried to scrub it clean but finally given up.

Luckily, I didn't actually need to go to the bathroom.

I searched the room quickly, looking for anything that resembled a camera or mic. *Nothing.*

The mirror over the sink looked wobbly and warped as I stared back at my own reflection. Finally, I shook off my fears and flashed myself with a determined grin. *I can do this. I owe it to my viewers, but mostly, I owe it to the victims of the Beechwood Massacre, who never got the justice they deserved.*

Carefully, I reached up and loosened my ponytail, then slid the thick, black scrunchie onto my wrist. My raven-colored hair fell, crinkled, to my shoulders. I lifted my scrunchie-laden wrist to my lips.

"I hope you all are getting this. I'm in the bathroom of Beechwood Castle, the site of the grisly mass murders that occurred in 1996," I spoke quietly, trying to muffle my voice behind the thick oak doors of the bathroom.

The moment that packet of waivers and the NDA arrived in the mail, I knew I had to find a work-around. The whole point of going—besides the money and intrigue—was to find out what I could about the place of the murders and report my findings on the channel when I returned.

After hours of researching hidden cameras and audio devices, I'd reached out to my online friend, and fellow techie, Ben. Like me, he was obsessed with true crime, struggling with his mental health, and repelled by most people. I told him about my dilemma, and he had come up with a plan.

Since there was a good chance I'd be searched before entering the premises, there was no way I could walk in with a camera or audio recorder. Unless they were wearable and easy to disguise…

The tiny spy camera was embedded in my necklace, a small crescent moon and connected star around my neck, and the audio recorder was sewn inside my scrunchie. They weren't connected to a live feed, but it would provide excellent data for when I returned home, as long as I didn't lose or break the devices. Or get caught, I thought, uneasily. Ben had helped me with them, but now I was on my own—I couldn't let anything happen to my camera or recorder, and I definitely couldn't let anyone else find out about them.

Unfortunately, the camera was miniscule, and the footage was grainy—I'd tested it out at home before coming —but the audio recorder in my scrunchie worked flawlessly. So what if I'd used all of my savings to get them? I'd get all that money back when I completed the night, and hopefully in the future from ad money when my channel grew even larger than it already was...

"I will tell you more later, when I get to my room and I'm alone," I told my scrunchie, staring into the mirror at myself. It was risky, and once I uploaded the audio and visuals online, I'd be at major risk of getting sued since I signed those forms. But at that point, it wouldn't matter. I'd have a lot of people on my side, rooting for me...

Because the way I saw it, someone brought us here for a reason. Not some simple psychological experiment or chance at reality TV, but something more sinister and shocking. It had to be related to those murders...

I could feel it deep in my bones.

Chapter Nine

Lolly

I t was the drawings that brought me here, back to this place of nightmares. The longer I thought about it, and the harder I studied those drawings, the more certain I became—I'd left them behind on the night of the murders. They weren't replicas; they were mine. And the only person who would have had access to them were the cops and personnel who responded to the crime scene, or the killer himself.

I'd assumed it might be the killer, taunting me after all these years ... because all of the cops who "worked" the murders were either dead or retired. What reason would they have for holding onto my drawings all this time, and then sending them to me now?

But now I realized my assumptions from before were wrong. Because now, I was sitting at a table with Rad fucking Williams, that pudgy, old cop who killed that kid and never even tried to solve my friends' murders. I was more convinced than ever that it was him who had sent me the drawings. Who else could it have been?

Rad Williams had my drawings all this time and he sent them to me, but why? Is he the one who arranged this whole thing? Why the hell did I agree to come here?!

I should have been at home, taking care of my daughter and my dad. But instead, I'd chosen to come, leaving my chipper Aunt Julie in charge of my most precious cargo in life. My father's sister, Julie, had been begging to come visit for months now, but every time she showed up she just looked down her nose at me and lectured me on how I needed to take better care of Dad.

Leaving Dad and Sadie with Aunt Julie while I came here to figure things out had seemed like a good idea at the time. But now that I was here, with Rad of all people! I felt furious and regretful. Why did I leave my daughter to come play this game, or whatever this was?

I knew each and every face at the table. Rad, obviously. But I also knew that strange chick from YouTube, "Stabby Staci" as they called her, and the famous true crime writer, Penelope Jewel, was here as well. I read the news about that pervert Cornelius's arrest in our local paper, and of course I knew Bonnie Black as well. Bonnie looked strange and grandmotherly at the head of the table, wearing those old-fashioned clothes and eccentric costume jewels, but she was only a few years ahead of me in school. Bonnie had run off at the end of high school, leaving Rock Hill, and then she'd come back with a druggie boyfriend and a newborn baby. I remembered when she got locked up on fraud charges, and I knew about her family history in the area. The Blacks were odd people, psychics and witchy folk. Bonnie and I had never been friends in school, but we shared some acquaintances when we were young. Her being here made no sense to me … what sort of purpose would she serve for this documentary, or whatever the hell this was?

Speaking of documentaries, we'd had no formal interviews. There were no cameramen in sight, and not even one single visible security camera that could be spotted by the naked eye.

Something about this didn't feel right. It didn't from the get-go, and it certainly didn't when those drawings turned up, but now I couldn't shake off the feeling of danger in the air.

From the moment my Uber had entered the windy back roads leading into the forestry, that cold sense of dread returned. Thoughts from that night, when my friends were murdered, were often scattered and random—me, always waking up on the edge of a dream, unsure if it was a memory or something my head and trauma had created all by itself.

The trees looked taller and thicker, but when I came through those gates, the castle itself looked harmless. Not this scary, dark monster hovering in the forest that I remembered, but just a pile of limestone and dirt. Birds were chirping, frogs croaked. The whole place looked smaller than I remembered, but harmless.

But when that hostess, Mary Beth Penner, led us inside and the doors locked behind us, it all came rushing back to me…

The foyer where six of us gathered by our host, was the same big empty room we used to sit around and drink booze in.

The walls had been covered and repaired by someone; the dirt floor looked cleaner than before … but this was the same old room. We'd chased each other through those pitch-dark hallways; no electricity available in the abandoned castle back then…

Now, the walls seemed to close in around me, the ceiling creaking and groaning overhead. And I knew it was probably all in my head, but I could swear that I smelled it —that tinge of death and decay in the air. The sweet, putrid scent of blood and bodily fluids that was in the air on the night that all my friends died…

This place was rundown and scary back then, but mostly … it was a place to get away from the other scary things in our lives. Our families, the pressures of school, the ills of adolescence…

We played tag like children down the halls and corridors of Beechwood Castle, and we fucked around like adults, drinking and kissing. Touching and fighting.

Monica was the only other girl who came. The boys were Thomas and Mike. I never felt close to any of them; I know that's not what you're supposed to say after someone dies, especially if they die young and tragically. But they weren't close friends to me, just a group of kids who hung around together during the summer months. They were people to have fun with, people to forget about … but now, I'd never forget their faces. Or the way they sounded when they died.

I liked Monica the most in our group; she wasn't the nicest girl and she acted differently when we were alone versus when we were with the boys, but she was fun sometimes.

Monica was the first to die. It was her screaming that brought us all outside, and that's when I saw him—the killer with the mask and his ax. Monica's throat hacked so deeply that her head was almost severed. It was that moment, frozen in time … that I remembered most. Because what happened after, when the rest of us scattered and ran, like ashes in the wind…that part of the story is a murky, fever dream that I never wanted to return to.

All I knew was that I was lucky to be alive, and here I was—back at the place that almost killed me. I should leave now. Fuck the money and fuck all these people. Who cared if I never unraveled this mystery of who sent the drawings?! I could live with that, but I couldn't live knowing that my daughter would have to grow up without a mother, especially considering her father was a deadbeat who took off right after I learned I was pregnant.

"I'm ready to go check out my room and settle in. This food has left me feeling … strange," Bonnie said, her words barely more than whispers.

"Me too," Cornelius said, scooting back in his chair. He

looked too big for it, like when Alice ate the "Eat Me" cake, arms and legs outgrowing the space around her...

"Wait." I leaned forward in my seat and lifted the untouched bowl of bread in the center of the table. While the rest of my fellow housemates had been chatting, staring, and eating, I'd noticed the corner of an envelope sticking out from under the bowl in the middle of the table.

"Mary Beth Penner told us that there would be instructions after dinner, and here they are," I said, picking up one envelope, only to discover another, smaller one, hidden beneath that one.

"There are two envelopes there resting in the center of the table. Our instructions," Staci spoke loudly from across the table, seemingly talking to herself, or no one. She was holding her hand in front of her face, her scrunchie practically in her mouth.

"I'll read the instructions aloud," Cornelius said, suddenly swiping the card from my hands.

Chapter Ten

Cornelius

"**S**orry," I told the woman named Lolly, giving her a sheepish look as I ripped the seal on the first envelope. "I get a little impulsive when I'm excited," I said.

"So we've heard, asshole," Rad, the ex-cop, gave me a death glare from across the table. The woman named Lolly shot him a dirty look, even dirtier than the one she'd given me when I took the card out of her hands. It was obvious that she and the cop had some sort of past relationship; the cop seemed protective and concerned about her, whereas she seemed like she was ready to punch his lights out. Either way, I didn't care. Their drama wasn't important to me—figuring out why I was selected to come here and winning the money to start my new life was my only concern from here on out. If my housemates thought I was a creep or perv, no matter. By this time next week, I'd either be long gone to somewhere tropical surrounded by hot girls in bikinis, or I'd be starting a new job with the owner of the Beechwood estate.

I slid a single thin slip of paper out of the envelope and read it slowly for my housemates:

"In your rooms, each of you will find individual letters that were personally left there for you. You may choose to share the contents of those letters with your fellow houseguests, or you may keep the contents to yourself. Like so much of this experience, the choice to share information will be yours, and yours alone. After dinner, you may explore the house and the grounds as you wish or retire to your individual rooms for a break. The only part of the property you may not access is the tower. It has been sealed off for safety reasons. Please be sure to meet back for drinks this evening at ten o'clock."

"That's it? That's all it says?" Lolly said, her voice angry and exasperated. Although the woman was attractive, the fact that she was always frowning annoyed me. Would it hurt to smile every once in a while?

"We still have the other envelope to read," I said, reaching for it. But before I could take it from the center of the table, that old, smartass bag of bones, Penelope Jewel, snatched it up.

"I expected you to have faster hands, seeing that you're a perv and all. I'll take it from here," she told me, opening the second letter.

Chapter Eleven

Penelope

For the first time since this whole event started, I could feel my intrigue piquing.

The second envelope was smaller than the first, and the pristine, typed letters were smaller too. I pushed my chair back and stood, reading its contents aloud for my fellow housemates:

"Per the guidelines you received, each of you has the opportunity to win a portion of the million-dollar prize pool. But here are a couple of things you do not know. Number one…" I cleared my throat, looking at the ghoulish faces around the table, slowing down for effect.

"This isn't an author reading at the bookstore, Penelope. Can you get on with it, please?" Staci, the wannabe YouTube detective, blurted out.

Annoyed, I continued: "Number one … if any of your

fellow houseguests forfeit their share of the prize pool, then their portion of the winnings will be added back to the total pool. When one of you leaves, the others benefit by increasing their percentage of the total amount."

More money for those who stay when others leave. Not surprising … but also quite boring. I moved on to the next numbered line.

"Number two. And this is all that is left to read…" I said, skimming the final line of instructions and raising a brow.

I could feel my houseguests shifting in their chairs, growing antsy. I took my time, reading it to myself first. I always did enjoy creating a little suspense.

"Come on, Penelope," Lolly growled.

"All of you are traitors," I said, surprising myself as I stumbled over the words. "But only one of you is an impostor."

One of my housemates gasped, but I went on: "Be the first to correctly identify the impostor who wasn't invited, and you will receive an additional sum of 500,000 dollars added to your prize earnings. But be warned. If you guess incorrectly, you must leave the premises immediately and forfeit all of your money. When you are ready to guess, you will enter the library. On the desk, you will find six envelopes and six slips of paper. Print your name on the back of the envelope, then print the name of the supposed impostor on the slip of paper and seal it within. Place your guess inside the top drawer and close it."

"Five hundred extra g's? That's insane. Whoa,"

Cornelius breathed, leaning over the table with his gangly limbs and looking around to get the other's reactions.

"What else does it say on there?" Rad, the retired cop asked. He was leaning back in his chair, arms crossed tightly over his chest. The man looked perpetually weary, and I had to wonder why in the hell he'd been chosen to come here besides his link to the past crime.

"That's it. That's all it says," I said, placing the card back on the table next to the first one. "Sounds like this night finally got a little interesting," I shrugged, re-taking my seat.

Chapter Twelve

Bonnie

W hen you make your money conning others, you get pretty good at spotting other cons ... and nothing about this latest development sat right with me.

More money? That was all this was about? I didn't buy it.

There wasn't one single, visible camera on the premises. No paid actors ... no cameraman.

Who is watching and who is benefiting from this whole charade? I couldn't help wondering.

"I'm going to my room," I said, rising to my feet on shaky legs. If my houseguests heard me, they didn't let on. They were talking wildly among themselves, accusing one another of being an impostor...

"I'm going..." I said again, to no one, walking toward the kitchen. The doors to the kitchen were old-fashioned, creaky swinging doors that filled me with a strange sense of déjà vu as I pushed through them.

"Oh." I startled at the sight of Mary Beth Penner, our self-proclaimed hostess. She appeared to have been listening from behind the door. Her cheeks reddened, and she stepped back and smoothed the front of her blouse.

"I was just leaving for the guesthouse," she told me, her cheeks red with embarrassment. "The caterers have all packed up, they're just waiting to clear the table."

Mary Beth appeared to be around my age, maybe forty or fifty, but there was something so young and fragile about her, like a scared little girl playing dress-up in a businesswoman's clothes.

"Alright," I said, wearily. My head was throbbing, and my thoughts were murky – bombarded by bad vibes, I couldn't tell if the uneasy feelings were coming from the people around me, or the house itself.

"I'm trying to find the second floor, so I can go to my room," I said, uneasily.

"Ah." Mary Beth stood up straighter, at ease with a question she could answer. "You'll go back out through the dining hall, collect your bag in the front room, and then take a right down the east corridor. You will see the staircase at the end of the hall. It's impossible to miss."

"Okay," I said, hesitating. "Do you know who brought us here?" I asked, staring into her eyes. She had refused to tell us earlier, but now that I had her alone, maybe I could convince her to talk.

"I..."

"Hey there!" Staci, that young YouTuber poked her head through the doors. "Looking for my room."

"Here. Let me escort you both before I take my leave," Mary Beth said, breaking eye contact with me.

Disappointed, I followed her and Staci back through the dining area, where our fellow guests were still sitting around the table, passing around the envelopes and talking in hushed voices. Mary Beth waited as Staci and I collected our bags and then led us over to the entrance of a pitch-black hallway that veered off from the living room. Despite the early evening hour, there was very little natural light coming through from outside. The old stone corridor looked like the entrance to hell.

Shuddering, I couldn't shake the feeling that I'd been here before—standing, waiting, preparing to enter...

"There's the stairs," Mary Beth said shakily, pointing at the end of the hall. There was a dark room on one side of the hallway, and a narrow set of stone stairs at the end of it. "I think you all can find it from here, yes?" For the first time, it became clear what our hostess was trying so hard to hide—she was afraid. Afraid of this place, maybe even afraid of us.

"Thanks!" Staci said, pushing past us. She was certainly eager to get upstairs to her room. She, too, was hiding something. Perhaps we all were. I turned back to our hostess to ask more questions, but Mary Beth Penner was gone, as though she couldn't get away from me fast enough. For a moment, I was overcome by an eerie sensation—that she had never been here at all, just another phantom haunting my real life as they did in my dreams...

Any answers I wanted to learn about this place or our reasons for coming, I would have to uncover all on my own.

Now, I found myself alone in the long dark hallway. Staci must have gone upstairs. The air around me smelled earthy and untouched, like wet concrete on a hot, rainy summer day. As I moved through the hallway, I peeked in the random doorway, expecting to find another room. Instead, it was another stony hallway, filled with the kind of darkness that overwhelms and is the thing of nightmares. The kind of darkness light can't penetrate. *The tunnel from my dreams.*

Shivering, I gripped my bag in my hands and made my way toward the stairs, hoping Staci wasn't too far ahead of me. As quickly as I'd wanted to get away from my fellow houseguests, these creepy, cold walls were closing in on me ... a different sort of dark vibe I didn't want to mess with.

This was a bad place. *It's evil, can you feel it?* I imagined a voice saying in my ear. Often, I liked to imagine the voices belonged to my mother and the mother before her; but there was something wispy and strange about the voice this time —like the speaker had ill intentions...

The staircase itself was narrow but sturdy, the stairs made of thick, jagged slabs of cut limestone. As I ascended, the stairs twisted and turned sharply, taking me higher and higher to reach the next floor...

I couldn't shake off a dizzying sensation, a thickness in

my skull. *What if there was poison in the food they fed you?* said the voice again, a gleeful lull in its tone.

When I reached the second-floor landing and discovered it was well lit with yellow bulbs, I gave a sigh of relief. On either side of the hallway, there were several doors. I brushed past them, running the tips of my fingers over their wooden surfaces, and thin, placards on the front of most that contained the names of my fellow houseguests.

I stopped at the last door on my right—Staci's room. She must have already gone inside, because she had closed it behind her. The door across from hers, on the other side of the hallway, belonged to me.

The door creaked as I turned the knob and stepped inside.

I don't know what I'd been expecting—a fancy, old-fashioned bed or a dresser? This room contained none of that. A rolled-up sleeping bag sat in a dusty corner, and that was it.

Unlike the downstairs, which had been lightly furnished by the new owner, this room looked vacant and forgotten … as though it hadn't been touched or entered in years…

Standing on the tips of my toes, I caught a glimpse out the barred window. From here, I had a view of the side of the property—just a wall of thick trees, and in the distance, I could see the silver links of the gates and fence lining the north side of the property.

"Penelope Jewel will be thrilled about this sleeping set-up," I muttered, unrolling my sleeping bag on the floor. As soon as the roll was unwound, I found a personal letter addressed to me hidden inside it.

Most of my housemates were probably hoping for clues about the impostor, but all I needed was an explanation— who brought us here and why? And where are the cameras?

Hoping for answers but expecting none, I set my duffel bag on the sleeping bag and took a seat on top of it to read my letter.

It was a simple cardboard piece of paper inside the envelope, with only one single sentence written on it:

Your daughter is here in the house.

Chapter Thirteen

Rad

While the others departed for their respective bedrooms on the second floor, I took the opportunity to explore. Beyond the main foyer and dining hall, I found a mostly un-usable kitchen space, a bathroom that smelled more like an outhouse than an indoor john, and the aforementioned "library".

The library was not really a library at all—just a cold empty chamber with a built-in, concrete nook, which contained a couple dozen old books inside it. The only furniture in the room was a small, antique desk. On it, I found empty envelopes and small slips of blank paper, along with a fountain pen that had a ninety-nine-cent Dollar Tree sticker still attached to it.

An impostor among us…

Most importantly: who brought us here? A question I'd

been wondering ever since that announcement went out over the radio wires.

I had no use for this room—sure, I could use 500,000 dollars in addition to my one-sixth share for staying the night, but that wasn't my reason for coming. Not the main one anyway...

Back in the kitchen and dining hall, I found my small overnight bag where I'd left it in the corner and made my way down the central hallway. Instead of going upstairs, I decided to explore the other room along the way. Only, it wasn't a room at all ... just a long dark tunnel that looked endless, and apparently had no lighting mechanisms in sight.

Lucky for me, I'd brought one approved personal item—a small, but stealthy, flashlight. It only made sense—if I couldn't bring my gun with me, at least I'd have the flashlight to help me get around if need be.

I tucked my bag in my armpit and used my other hand to hold the flashlight and light the way.

The tunnel was cold, dank, and as I made my way down it, I could hear sounds coming in from outside. Birds singing in the distance, and the soft pitter patter of light rainfall.

This hallway was solid and unused, bits of lichen and moss growing on its slick floors, like witch's hair sprouting through the cracks. As the long tunnel went on and on, I could feel panic growing in my chest. Over the years, I'd had very few incidents on the force that caused anxiety, but this was like the stuff of a cop's nightmares—moving through the dark, not knowing what might lie ahead, or behind you…

Just as I was about to turn back and retrace my steps, I saw a flash of light up ahead. I kept going, following the slip of light and the sounds of the forest … and was stunned when I reached a wide-open exit—almost like a gaping mouth—that led to the back of the property.

The sunlight and fresh air hit me like a real, tangible force, and I dropped my bag on the ground and looked around me, taking it all in. There was a small drizzle of rain in the air, but it felt refreshing despite the time of year.

Apparently, I wasn't the only one with the idea of exploring while the others went to their rooms… Lolly stood only ten feet ahead, staring into the murky depths of a greenish-brown pool that looked like it used to be a swimming hole, or fishpond, but it was too unclear to tell which.

"You again, huh? Seems like you're following me," she said, giving me a dark glare over her shoulder, then refocusing on the water in front of her.

"Not following you. Just exploring, and trying to get some fresh air," I said. "Did you know this tunnel led out here?"

Lolly waited several long seconds to answer me, and I stepped up beside her at the pool. I could remember exploring the crime scene all those years ago, but I didn't remember this. In fact, I barely remembered *her* back then—I was so hell-bent on taking down a suspect and making a name for myself.

"Yeah, I remembered. I'm surprised that I did, but I did… I guess its just muscle memory…" Lolly said, staring into the water.

There was nothing to see, really, the water reflectionless and dark. It could have gone down a hundred feet, and I wouldn't know the difference. But across the surface, flickers of tadpoles danced across the water. If not tadpoles, then maybe mosquitoes.

"That water is disgusting," I said, stepping back from the edge.

"It used to be pretty clean. We swam here sometimes, on hot days. Me and the other kids who hung out here when I was young," Lolly said, vaguely. "Why the hell did you come here?" she said, abruptly turning to stare at me.

Seeing her like that, eyes hard and colorless, brought back memories of her as a girl. I did remember; only, I'd tried my hardest to forget.

Unlike other victims of violent crime, Lolly had seemed cold and hard, unwilling to talk much and unfazed by what had happened to her friends. Probably just in shock.

There was talk in the town, gossipy old ladies trying to blame her and the other teenagers … but I knew it wasn't her that did it. The person who hacked her friends up with an ax was stronger than a bird-boned, thirteen-year-old girl with an attitude problem, it didn't take a genius to figure that out. But still, people always like to talk … and to victim blame when it suits them.

"I'm here for the same reason you are, Lolly. Because someone invited me here. Any idea who that might be?"

"Questions. Questions … now you and your people want to ask me questions," Lolly said, dully, sticking the tip of her combat boot in the water. I had this flashing thought, that she might fall in and sink to the bottom, never surfacing again…

"We asked you lots of questions back then, too. So, I don't understand what you mean," I said. I looked around us, the thick trees of the forest … not a person or camera in sight. This makes no sense. Why were we even here?

"Well, not enough to find out who killed them. You were too focused on that Reeks kid, and he wound up dead because of it," Lolly said, bitterly.

I winced. I should have expected this, coming here … that someone would bring it up. But I hadn't expected to come face to face with Lolly Andrews either, the final girl of the massacre that happened all those years ago…

What are the odds? Certainly, our reunion here is no accident.

"You're right. I thought it was Reeks back then, and part of me still does. I had good reason to suspect him. He'd been hanging around the woods, watching you all. And masturbating too … did you know we found semen?"

"Please. I don't want to hear an old man say 'semen'," Lolly said, raising her hand in protest.

"Well, you're not that young anymore either, Lolly. I guess time has aged us both," I said. As soon as the words were out of my mouth, I knew they were all wrong. You should never tell a woman she looks old. But time had been rough on Lolly; the lines of her face were drawn; she looked even more birdlike and shrunken, a ghost of her former self.

"Fuck you," she spat, suddenly shoving past me and heading back for the entrance to the tunnel.

I considered running after her, asking more questions … but what was the point? Even if she knew more about who had brought us here, I was the last person she would tell.

"Lolly, wait!"

I didn't expect her to turn around, but she did.

"I'm sorry about your friends, I truly am. I know that you must miss them," I said.

"You don't know shit. You never did," Lolly said, disappearing through the wide-open jaws of the tunnel.

Chapter Fourteen

~SEVEN O'CLOCK~

Staci

I watched them from my careful corner—a shady, narrow gap between two trees. The cop and the girl, they interested me more than the others. *Their presence makes sense here.*

There was clearly tension between them, angry words exchanged at the side of the sludge pool. I held back, waiting and watching, hoping some or all of it was being recorded on my hidden audio device. My hopes were low though; as they were nearly ten feet away from where I hid, and the persistent pitter patter of rainfall from the sky obscured not only my audio, but visual too.

While Bonnie and the hostess had hesitated in the main hallway before the stairs, I'd slipped off down the hallway to explore. I wasn't the only one with that idea, obviously.

The impostor.

As soon as Penelope had read that part aloud, I'd considered fessing up ... telling my fellow housemates all about my invitation, and my failure to tell my channel's co-host, Jan.

But the moment had passed, and like some of the others here, I was holding back secrets for myself. Lolly Andrews certainly was...

I'd done my research on the Beechwood Massacre before coming: three teenagers killed with an ax in 1996. One sole survivor: Lolly Andrews. She claimed that she barely saw the killer, just a person who appeared to be male in a ski mask.

Like so many others before me, I thought that story sounded a little too convenient ... a little too cinematic. And no one had ever explained why Lolly was left unharmed, or who the killer might have been if not the Rock Hill's sheriff's main culprit, Bobby Reeks, who was taken out prematurely, thanks to our very own housemate and former cop, Rad Williams.

Rad stood, poolside, watching Lolly go. He looked haunted by the woman, and I wondered if there was a part of him that still saw the girl when he looked at her...

Slowly, Rad turned, head down and shielded from the rain, and disappeared back through the tunnel with a handy flashlight in his hand. I should have thought of bringing a flashlight for one of my personal items. But I hadn't expected the house to feel so dark, or for the tunnel to be so long and lightless, leading away from the castle.

I waited several minutes, letting the cold rainy mist

blow over me. It was warm for November, but somehow, the world seemed darker and colder here. A perpetual cloud already shielding the sun from where I stood next to the castle; a solemn cast of darkness all around me.

I followed Rad's lead and made my way back through the tunnel. Our host, Mary Beth Penner, had mentioned candles in the kitchen, so I decided to gather some of those before retiring to my room, in spite of Mary Beth saying that it was against the rules. I might need them later.

Chapter Fifteen

Lolly

I thought that if I went outside, followed those old familiar twists and turns, and the wet, earthy smells of the tunnel, that I could drown out the screams.

Because it's not the memories of their faces ... those mangled bodies. No, that's not the part that haunts me most. It's the sounds they made when they were dying ... screams so desperate and wild. So raw and animalistic.

Screams I chose to ignore in order to save myself.

But if I had to do it all over again, would I do it any differently? *No, I don't think I would.*

I'm alive and they're not. There has to be a reason for that ... that has to count for something, doesn't it?

My friends' screams live in the whispers between the trees; they're carried through the air and spread by the wind. Whether inside or outdoors, there's no escaping what happened that awful night.

Their screams live deep inside of me. There's no point running from them anymore…

At home, it was easy to forget—my days were structured by tasks and responsibilities. Taking care of Dad. Seeing Sadie off to school. Working a shift at Home Depot. Skipping lunch so I could leave an hour early to get home to dad. Cooking dinner, washing clothes. Helping with homework. Shower, sleep, repeat.

But every once in a while, when I caught a break in between the muscle memory motions of my life, I thought I could hear them. And out here, in these woods … this castle … well, the screams hadn't stopped since my Uber had made the sharp left turn onto Clifty and entered the dark patch of tree-lined road that led to the castle in Beechwood.

As a kid, I'd walked here, mostly. Or, sometimes, caught a ride with Thomas. He was the oldest of our group. So many days here after school, and then occasionally, late at night when we could sneak away from our parents. The others struggled with it … excuses and lies. But never me. My parents never knew when I was leaving. There were nights when I arrived to meet the others, then waited at the creepy castle all by myself. On a few of those nights, the others never even showed up.

The first couple of times it was frightening, but then I started to enjoy it. The echoing walls of the empty, graffiti-covered stone building, and the dark hush of the trees … even the bugs and animals were mostly quiet. I drew in my notebook, creating some of my best artwork ... my body hopped up on fear.

I stopped feeling afraid of this place, after a while. I wandered the abandoned hallways, pretending I was someone else—not a princess in a castle, but a warrior or a witch. Someone who was alone, but never lonely. A girl without a drunk for a father, or a mom who was always sick.

I'd sit by that dark pool outside, trying to see my reflection by the light of the moon. I wanted to see myself drawing, see if I looked like a witchy, artist type. But I could never see it, the pool so black and filled with muck, even back then, that it looked like a portal to another world ... or like something heinous might come crawling out of it.

Since I couldn't see my reflection, I sometimes liked to imagine there was someone out there, watching from between the trees. Someone watching over me, someone who had my back and didn't think I was a weird loner girl like most of the kids did at school.

Even my "friends" at the castle thought I was strange. Closer to each other than to me, I was always made to feel like the outside of our small four-person gang. At school, they mostly ignored me.

When we were all together, nights were fun. We'd run around the castle, playing hide and seek. Or drinking stale beer out of cans and puffing on our parents' Marlboros.

It was the only time I fit in. Now, decades later, I could see that it wasn't my sparkling personality that drew them to me—it was my access to things. My father's liquor cabinet, my mother's money she'd forgotten was hidden in the space between her mattress and frame … and my willingness to try anything, to be whoever they asked me to be.

Yes, this place used to be a comfort. It used to be fun… but that all ended.

This place didn't bring me solace. Now, it was just the place of nightmares, the murder house in the woods.

And I hadn't picked up a sketchbook or drawing pencil in years.

At the top of the twisty staircase, I found a door with my name on it—the first door on the left. Relieved to be close to the staircase in case I needed to run away from here, filled me with a small sliver of comfort.

I can do this. I can make it through the night, and hopefully find out more about who sent those drawings…

Inside my room, I was disappointed to find a single sleeping bag rolled up in the corner, but I *was* relieved to find a good, sturdy lock on the door. I locked myself in and placed my backpack on the floor beside the bedroom door.

First, I walked through the entire room, looking for cameras or some sort of indication that I was being spied on here. But there was nothing.

I'd spent time in some of these upstairs rooms as a kid, including this one. But most of the time I spent with the others was done outside or sitting in the front room downstairs.

But I knew that one thing was different … the walls up here, just like the walls downstairs, had been covered in thick, globby layers of paint. Although it made sense that a new owner would paint over the rough, graffitied walls of an abandoned building, the paint in here didn't look modern or new. It was chipped and scabby, bubbling up in certain sections, as though it had been like this for decades.

Perhaps someone painted here long ago, after the murders. A clean-up crew or the city of Rock Hill. Who knew? It didn't seem like a recent update though.

Slowly, I ran my fingers over the paint ... searching. *There.* The words were still there, only hidden, like jagged artifacts, hidden beneath layers of paint. I could feel them, trace them with my fingers ... just like I could still hear and feel the childlike screams. Just like how I could still smell the scent of blood in the air that night, even taste it...

I knew what the paint was covering. Big, angry letters that spelled out the words:

Fuck all of you. I hate you.

I knew that because I'd written those words in this very room, so long ago...

Trembling, I pulled myself away from the wall and started unrolling my sleeping bag.

That's when an envelope fell out of the bedding and hit the dusty, stone floor at my feet.

I'd nearly forgotten ... we were each supposed to get a personal letter according to the notes left on the dining table in the main hall for all of us to read at lunch.

Maybe this letter will offer some answers ... like why I'm here and who sent me those drawings. Did the aforementioned 'impostor' send those drawings to my house?

I couldn't see the "impostor"—if indeed the impostor and sender of the drawings were the same person—being anyone other than Officer Rad Williams, since he was the only one directly related to me and the case … but then again, the others were all local. They could know my story, have access to this place before tonight… You never really know your neighbors.

Like the letter I'd received in the mail and the letter on the dining table, this one was sealed in a thick, cream envelope. My name was written in bold, black cursive on the back.

Still shaky, I took a seat on the hard floor and ripped the letter open. I gasped when I read what was written inside it.

The words mimicked a terrifying nursery rhyme I vaguely remembered from my youth; a haunting rhyme based on the real-life story of an infamous child killer in the late 1800s who was accused of using an ax to kill her family. But Lizzie Borden's name had been replaced with mine…

> *Lolly Andrews took an ax*
> *And gave her friends forty whacks.*
> *When she saw what she had done,*
> *She gave her best friend forty-one.*

Chapter Sixteen

Cornelius

From the moment I stepped foot on the property, I felt like I was already hired for the job. I would expand the windows to let in more light—the place was horribly gloomy! Knock down some of those oddly placed walls that turn the space into a maze of corridors; instead, it could be more open and airier ... a modern-day, chic version of a castle in the woods. Some rich fuck would scoop it up and pay millions for the house and land, after I was done with the work.

But the wheels in my brain were turning again now, switching direction, and there was a heated excitement building in my chest that began right after dinner... It was the mention of all that money that really changed things for me. One hundred and fifty grand plus another five hundred on top of it?! That was enough to say, "Fuck you", to any future employers, and use the money as a start-up for my *own* construction business. Screw working for anyone else!

Six hundred thousand dollars wouldn't make me mega-rich, not in these tumultuous, economic times. But it would be enough to pick up and go and get something started on my own. I could be my own boss ... no more coffee-breath losers breathing down my neck. No more lectures. No more uptight people treating a man like a monster just for getting a little excited over a naked, hot woman in the window. She was standing there for a reason—she obviously wanted the attention I gave her, but now I was getting distracted again...

I'd told my wife and kids that I was spending the next couple of days at a conference in Philly. The topic: biophilic design. The look she gave me—a mixture of disbelief, disgust, and outright disdain—was enough to solidify my position. Our marriage was over, along with my chances of having a successful career in this town. Screw Rock Hill!

A chance to meet the new owner of the Beechwood property presented an exciting opportunity ... but the chance of winning all that money, and going off on my own? The more I thought about it, the more I liked my chances and that option better.

All I had to do was unmask the impostor and be the first to do it.

The sleeping bag set-up was underwhelming, but I didn't plan on sleeping tonight anyway. As I unrolled it and spread it out on the floor, I came across a formal letter, written specifically for me:

Dear Mr. Cornelius Jones,

I'm a great admirer of your recent work and I was sorry to hear about your recent legal troubles. As stated in the group announcement, an impostor walks among you. One of your houseguests is not supposed to be here and I challenge you to uncover who that houseguest is. With your methodical mind and impressive background, you are certain to stand a good chance at being the winner of the extra prize pool funds. There is another letter containing clues to the impostor's identity, but first you must find it. There was a rule set forth in the beginning, about where houseguests are allowed to go, and which area is off-limits. Luckily, you don't seem like a man who always follows the rules. That will be to your advantage today, if you really want to win the extra prize.

Warm regards,

Beechwood LLC, et al.

A rush of adrenaline coursed through me as I tucked the letter inside my suitcase of belongings and removed the only personal items I'd brought with me—my felt tip pen and drafting pad. I didn't have any other tools—no scale or drafting dots—but all I needed was a quick sketch, and my 'methodical mind' as the writer had called it.

With no tables to draft, I got to my knees and began drafting a quick, and slightly messy, blueprint of the castle. There hadn't been enough time to fully explore the house or grounds yet, but I knew just from eyeballing the place on the way in, and looking at old pictures online before I arrived, exactly where entry to the tower should be.

The writer had mentioned that I didn't always like following the rules—which wasn't exactly true, but whatever—and had made mention again about the rule regarding guests not being permitted tower access. Earlier, it was mentioned that the tower had been "sealed off" for safety concerns.

That must be where the clues I needed were hidden.

As I finished my drawing—not to scale, but oh well—it suddenly occurred to me that the other houseguests might have received the exact same letter. Or perhaps, they were being led to other rooms for clues.

I couldn't let anyone else unmask the impostor before I did!

Single-mindedly, I tucked the drawing in the pocket of my trousers and slipped out into the hallway. The second-floor corridor was silent; all the doors with the guests' names labelled shut tight. Were they all in their rooms, or still downstairs, I wondered.

I stopped, listened. There were sounds coming from downstairs, the shuffling of feet and the bouncing echo of voices below. I wasn't a religious man, but I said a quick prayer anyway as I opened the door to that young chick named Staci's room. In a span of a few seconds on my walk to her door, I'd decided that if she was in there, I'd simply pretend I'd gone to the wrong room. She probably wouldn't believe me, but since they'd already labelled me as a "pervert", their opinion didn't matter anyway.

I was willing to step on a few toes—or many—if it

meant snatching the money before anyone else had a chance to.

When I opened the door to Staci's room and found it empty, I breathed a sigh of relief. Quickly, I locked her door behind me so I wouldn't be discovered and walked over to the sleeping bags on her floor.

Two bags were tightly rolled, but there was no sign of Staci's personal luggage. *She hasn't been up here in her room yet, which means she's probably coming soon. Must hurry!*

I moved to the far east corner of her room and began examining the wall with a keen eye.

Although the owner's letter to me had seemed formal, and certainly written by an academic of some sort, I now doubted that he—or she, I suppose—had any sort of formal training in architecture or structural design. I hadn't caught the mistake earlier today, but I did this time—the writer referred to the sealed off section as a "tower". But most people who have studied design like I have, know that little towers that don't reach all the way to the ground, are technically referred to as "turrets", not "towers".

Turrets are complex structures used in medieval times to create a projecting position for a lookout during times of military defense. They require a great deal of support, and usually require a corbel to serve as a bracket to hold them up. There was only one possible way to enter the turret from inside the castle—at the edge of the structure where it protruded—and that edge directly corresponded to the room assigned to Staci. That's how I knew where to go.

Another panicky thought rushed in—*what if she's already made it inside herself, and I'm too late?!*

But as I scanned the wall frantically, my eyes landed on the faux stone section of the wall. Someone had gone to a lot of trouble to make it look legit, and the pigments did give the phony veneer a stone-like look.

I pressed my hands to it, just to be sure. Indeed, a small portion of the exterior wall was filled with low-density foam and coated in a hard plastic layer. There was no mistaking this was the wall that concealed the entrance to the turret.

Now I just needed to get inside it.

Heart thumping in my chest, I felt all around the veneer stone edges, looking for some sort of lever, or way to easily get inside.

There had to be a way that didn't involve busting down the wall and going through it ... but if it came to that, I would do it. Five hundred thousand extra dollars was well worth the risk.

My wife thinks I'm an idiot and a perv but look at me now! I really do have a methodical brain because I figured this out in fewer than ten minutes!

All I needed now was a fast—or messy—way into the turret, so that I could reach the clue I needed to determine the impostor...

The smug smile vanished from my face as a loud scream ripped through the air. It was less of a scream, and more of a roar ... like a wild beast coming to attack me...

Chapter Seventeen

Penelope

The sleeping arrangements were less than ideal, but there was no way I'd be able to sleep in this drafty, dirty place tonight anyway. I considered my beautiful home I'd left behind for the night—Robert bringing me hot tea and me, at my computer working. Perhaps strolling in the garden again, or just napping in our four-poster bed. These days, naps were less of a luxury and more of a requirement for me...

Robert understood that, and he always took care of me. I should be home with him, and not this awful dirty place with its lame sleeping bag and dirt-covered, freezing cold floors...

I forgave Robert before I left. He shouldn't have held onto the letter so long, but I understood his motives. He had always been so unselfish and faithful; I had to give the man a little leeway when it came to mistakes.

Kicking aside the sleeping bag I went to my luggage. I'd packed a couple extra sets of clothes and some toiletries. But most importantly, I'd brought along paper and pencils so I could jot down notes for later.

Before leaving, I'd considered calling my agent and telling her the news but for now, I felt like keeping my plans to myself. Despite the literary world's lack of interest in dealing with me, or any of my recent true crime proposals, I had a feeling they might change their tune when they heard about the access I was being granted to the infamous site of the heinous Beechwood ax murders and some of the people who were directly involved in the crime case back in 1996.

It felt like fate that I was here. Although, I usually wasn't the suspicious type.

Right now, my main interest was getting some alone time with the girl ... the final girl, Lolly Andrews, the sole survivor of the Beechwood Massacre. I could understand not wanting to talk to the press all these years, but perhaps she would feel differently now about me. After all, she used to be a fan of my work...

All those years ago—it felt like only yesterday but, truly, it had been more than two decades past—Lolly was put under a big, bright spotlight. Questioned by police and photos snapped everywhere she went; she was just a young girl, too young to have to deal with all that. But it was my own name that caught my attention one night on the local news. Lolly Andrews was spotted at the local library less than a year after her friends' murders, an armful of true crime books caught on video.

Of course the press had a field day with that—as though reading true crime is a crime itself or means that someone has murderous thoughts. Ridiculous!

But I'd noticed one of my own books in her stack, and I felt a strange sense of pride. Back then, I thought I'd get to do the story. Coming off the heels of my recent success and being local to the area, it was certain that I should be the one to write it.

But then that prick Edward McCulty got the deal first, and I never got to pursue it.

Well, that is going to change now. And perhaps Lolly, or even Rad, would be willing to discuss the case with me.

I jumped at the sound of a low-pitched scream, almost like a growl coming through the hallway. I had no doubt— the angry outburst was coming from our very own final girl.

Chapter Eighteen

Bonnie

The room was spinning. My heart was the spoke, my head, a tilt-a-whirl. Nothing made sense anymore.

Your daughter is here in the house.

That's it; that's all my letter said. Either a cruel joke or a sick and twisted reunion, orchestrated to destroy. To destroy what's left of me ... what the prison system and the consequences of my poor decisions had left behind.

I folded the letter, again and again, until the square of paper was so tiny that it reminded me of Cecilia's hand ... the day she was born, that little bitty hand, curled into a mighty fist. She was strong. She was born with a full head of hair. And she looked right into my eyes, as though she could see deep within my soul, and I in hers.

The paper hit the floor as a long, strangled howl released into the hallway outside my locked door. *Cecilia? Is that you?*

I ran to the door, turned the lock, and burst into the hall. It was full of other houseguests.

"What's wrong?" I said, feeling the thick fog of anger in the air long before I realized from whom the string of shouts and growls were coming from.

Lolly.

"I want to know which one of you wrote this letter. Tell me the truth right now!" Lolly roared, her face beet-red, and her pupils dilated. I'd seen people this angry before ... but only behind the walls of prison. Women who had been abused, women who were full of red-hot rage with no way to cool it.

"Tell me now!" Lolly screamed again. One by one, she looked at our faces, her jaw flexing angrily through her cheek.

"Let me see," I said calmly, stepping between Penelope and Rad to reach her. "Please."

Carefully, I wrapped my hands over hers. Lolly's hands were shaking and for a brief moment, my body felt a flash of not only her rage, but also stone-cold fear. It was coursing through her whole body.

Gently, I pried Lolly's fingers apart and took the wadded-up note from her hands.

"Read it! What the hell does it say?" Cornelius shouted at me. He was standing all the way at the other end of the hallway, on the wrong side considering his room was much closer to the top of the stairwell.

I scanned the words of Lolly's letter; it only took a few seconds to recognize the horrific Lizzie Borden rhyme most of us remembered from our own childhoods. Only, someone had put their own twist on the words, making Lolly herself the focus. What a sick and twisted rhyme…

"I'm not reading it. I'll pass it around," I said, looking first to Lolly to make sure it was okay. But she stared at me blankly, as though she were looking straight through me.

"What's going on?" Staci said, suddenly popping up from the stairwell.

"Someone wrote something heinous and left it for Lolly to find. She's trying to figure out who it was," I told her, just as Rad snatched the note from my hands. Penelope leaned in to read it over his shoulder, and Staci edged down the hallway, closer, so she could catch a glimpse too.

"I'm sorry, Lolly. This is awful. I didn't write it," I said, trying to catch her eye. She still looked angry, but she needed some sort of response, reassurance from us. She needed something to cool down the burning coals of anger inside her.

As I observed the rock-hard look in her eyes, I was able to get a good read on her—she was soft as butter on the inside, but she'd learned how to build a shell. When she felt threatened or fearful, that shell came down hard around her. And right now, Lolly Andrews was impenetrable.

One by one, the others denied it too. A chorus of 'not me' and 'I didn't do it' rang out through the hall.

"I also received a strange letter," I said, my voice barely above a whisper. Lolly's eyes came back into focus, and she locked in on me, letting me in for the first time.

"What did yours say?" she asked, glancing down at my empty hands.

"I left it in my room when I heard you screaming..." I looked around at the others; they were all watching me, too, with interest. I wondered if they, too, got similar letters, alluding to their past, or secrets...

I hadn't planned on telling a soul about what my letter said, not until Lolly's admission. But now, it seemed, to me, that working together to solve this mystery was probably our best bet. Also, I wanted to know if the letter could possibly be true.

My daughter ... here in Rock Hill all this time, and I hadn't seen her since she was a little girl in my arms...

"When I was sentenced to prison, the state took away my baby daughter. She was less than a year old, not even out of diapers yet ... I never saw her again."

The others averted their eyes; people don't know what to say when you tell them something terrible, especially if it's something they think you probably deserved to have happened.

"My letter contained only one sentence. It said that my daughter is here in the house," I said, trying to keep my voice even and calm.

"But who? Who would do that to you?" Rad said, his expression perplexed. He shifted from foot to foot; *this one is a nervous one,* I thought. *A real soul on edge, unable to anchor himself to this world anymore…*

I cleared my throat. "If this is true, then there's only one person who fits the age … my Cecilia would be twenty-six next April," I said.

All eyes turned to look at the youngest in our group.

"It has to be you," I said, pointing a shaky finger down the hallway toward Staci.

Chapter Nineteen

Rad

Although Bonnie and Staci's (possible) predicament— *mother and daughter, really?*—was interesting, and confusing, my focus was still on Lolly. Those words, that dark and childish rhyme ... why would someone leave that for her in her room to find?

Of course it had crossed my mind back then that she could be the killer. It was unlikely—men almost always commit most crimes of that nature. And even those crimes committed by females ... rarely was a child of Lolly's age and stature capable of that kind of violence and gore.

Faces flashed before my eyes—the wide-open stare of Thomas Tartan, his arms and chest hacked up so badly that he looked like he'd been run through a meat grinder. Mike Wilcox, who took an ax to the back *and* also the front ... no doubt he was made to suffer, and he tried to stay on his feet. And Monica Collins … practically decapitated, the assailant swinging the ax again and again at her neck in the same area, committing violence way past the point of death…

Shuddering, I tried to step closer to Lolly. To talk quietly to her, alone, there in the hallway among the others.

"Don't fucking touch me," Lolly snarled, swinging her arms and elbows to keep me away.

I could understand why she hated me. I was a hot-shot rookie back then, with an arrogant attitude, and I'd fucked up the case right from the get-go. But I really did want to solve it, back then and still today. And I'd give anything to go back, do it all over again … take that younger version of me by the shoulders and shake some damn sense into him.

"We can all figure this out together," I said, holding up my hands to let her know I, indeed, would not touch her.

"I work better alone. Always have. I need some air," Lolly said, scooting around Bonnie, Penelope, and Staci. "And don't follow me," she warned, shooting a hard look at me over her shoulder, before disappearing down the stairwell.

I wanted to follow her because I was concerned. But I also wanted to know more. Maybe someone who knew something back then was trying to bring us here to resolve things now. Lolly certainly had enough anger to kill, if looks could kill, that is…

But before her friends were murdered, had she been an angry child? Was she really capable of whacking her friends, like the kiddish rhyme taunted?

I turned back to the others, tuning back into their conversation. The personal connection between Bonnie and Staci seemed like something completely different ... something totally unrelated, or was it?

Bonnie's speech was pressured: "It would have been a little over twenty years ago ... you see, my baby stayed with her father's family for a little while, but they wouldn't keep her permanently and then she went into the system. No one ever told me what happened to her. But I assumed, and hoped, she got far away from this town."

Staci had taken several giant leaps back from the frantic woman. She was shaking her head back and forth. "No, I'm sorry. It's not me ... I'm not your daughter, Bonnie."

"You aren't adopted?" Bonnie said. The fallen look on Bonnie's face was so plain to see, and raw with pain, that I felt a flinch of pain in my own chest. Unlike Bonnie, I'd never had any children of my own. Not because I didn't want them. My wife and I had trouble conceiving right from the start, and the shooting death caused by my error just added extra stress on her.

Sometimes, just walking along the street, I'd see a young person and wonder what my own child would look like, talk like ... if Kate and I had ever had one. She'd been gone a little over a year now, losing her battle to cancer. I missed her more than anything in this world.

"I'm not adopted," Staci said, still shaking her head.

"Well, no other guests here could even possibly be my daughter. This makes no sense..." Bonnie said. Penelope was watching her, eyes bright with interest. There was something so cold and mean in that writer's eyes, it made me uncomfortable. And her dark humor was so off-putting.

Cornelius was still standing at the end of the hallway, unwilling to join the group. It looked like he was thinking about sneaking away from us, but there was nowhere to go but past us if he wanted to reach his room or go downstairs.

Down below, I heard the loud thump of the front door slamming shut.

I hope Lolly really is just getting some air, and not leaving. I need answers before she leaves this estate…

"Maybe," Penelope said, clearing her throat, "the whole purpose of this exercise was to cause confusion and create drama among us group of six. If they're recording us, whoever they are, then this whole conversation makes for some interesting TV. Don't you think?"

"No. I don't think this is interesting at all. It's my life, Penelope, not some sort of daytime soap opera," Bonnie snapped.

"It's possible…" Staci said, chewing her lip and staring down at the floor.

"Possible you were adopted after all?" I asked, joining the conversation.

"No. Not me. That's the thing… Listen, I lied to all of you before. The letter I received in the mail wasn't for me, not specifically. Maybe your long-lost daughter is my co-host, Jan… I think it was she who was meant to be here, not me."

Bonnie gasped. "Where is this Jan person?"

Staci shrugged, sheepish. "I don't really know. At home, I guess. In her apartment in Rock Hill. I should have told her the truth about the letter. And I should have told all of you... I am the impostor," Staci said.

Chapter Twenty

~NINE O'CLOCK~

Staci

F ewer than forty-five minutes had passed since the confrontation upstairs, but I was still feeling shaken by it. All of it.

I'd been forced to confess—while my scrunchie recorder recorded it all—and tell them about my co-host, Jan. I couldn't include this part on my channel—it made me look bad. It made me look like a liar, once again, to my viewers.

"It's not certain that you're the impostor," Bonnie said, lifting her fingers in air quotes when she mentioned that term. "You said that the letter was addressed to your channel name, The Forgotten and the Lost, so technically that means you were probably both invited. So, not an impostor, but Jan is missing from our group…"

Bonnie was sitting right next to me on the sofa; I could smell lavender and mint in her hair, and something sweet on her breath. What I really wanted to do was run, get far away from these people … nothing about this experience so far was going as planned.

"Maybe you're right," I said, remembering something else. "I'm pretty sure they knew I was coming … I received the paperwork and sent it back to them with my name. If I weren't meant to be here instead of Jan, wouldn't someone have stopped me by now? But I'm still pretty sure Jan is who they wanted. She is the real face of the channel…"

"Jan," Bonnie pressed, trying to get closer to me again. "Can you tell me anything about her?"

I shifted farther away, pressing my hip against the armrest to get away from her.

"Not really. I mean, she's adopted. But I don't know many details. Jan is kind. She's smart … we used to be good friends," I said, a feeling of guilt and sadness blooming in my chest. It was wrong of me not to share the details with Jan, no matter how pissed at me she was before leaving. After all, she had every reason to be angry with me after I made up that whole audio recording to gain more attention for the crime case.

"I would love to meet her after this. I could even give her my portion of the money. She deserves it after what I did to her," Bonnie said. Her eyes were watching my every move, searing into my soul, and this time when she scooted closer to me, I had nowhere to go. She reached out and touched my arm.

"Thank you for telling me the truth," Bonnie said, her hands cold as ice on my forearm.

"No problem," I said, trying to pull away but Bonnie only gripped me harder.

"I hate to break up this lovely talk of family, but I'm famished, and I need to go get changed for our drinking hour soon," Penelope said, rising from the wing-backed chair.

The sun outside had dipped below the horizon, darkness sneaking up on us without us realizing it. Bonnie released her grip on me and moved farther down the couch. I sighed audibly with relief.

"Penelope, wait," I said, calling out to the snooty writer. She seemed cold and rude over dinner, and her response to Lolly and Bonnie's personal letters had been lukewarm at best.

"You never told us what was in your letter," I said, relieved to be talking to someone who wasn't Bonnie. But even from the corner of my eye, I could see her—feel her—watching my every movement.

"Ah, yes," Penelope said, freezing in the doorway by the hall. "It was impersonal, unlike the others. It just gave clues about who the impostor might be."

"What clues?" Rad said, turning away from his post at the window, where he'd been watching and waiting for Lolly to return from her angry stroll to "get some air".

"Wouldn't you like to know that?" Penelope sniffed.

"I don't care about the money. I just want to know who's behind this. And if that means identifying the impostor, and they're one and the same, then yes I would like to know.

And I'm pretty certain that we all agree it's not that Staci girl," Rad said, stiffly.

"What about you, Rad?" I said, taking in his beefy, world-weary exterior for the first time. He'd mostly been quiet over dinner, holding back until Lolly forced him to admit who he was, but I remembered reading about him back in the day while doing my crime research. He'd been a drinker and a hothead. Fairly new to the force, he'd gone way too far in his pursuit of local drug dealer, Bobby Reeks. Now, he seemed like a shell of that young man. Instead, he seemed tired and decidedly level-headed.

"I didn't get a personal note," Rad said, with a small shrug.

"You didn't get one? I wonder why…" Bonnie said, finally turning her attention from me to the former cop.

"I have no idea, but I hope to find out soon enough," Rad said, softly, turning back to the window.

When I looked back down the hallway, Penelope was gone. Back up to her room to get changed, I presumed. Lolly still hadn't returned, and Cornelius had slipped away right after the incident with Lolly's letter upstairs, not joining us in the living room for our group discussion. Cornelius claimed that he wanted to explore the castle's structure and rooms, but I wondered if that were really true. He and I were the only ones who hadn't shared information with the group about our personal clues…

As though he were thinking the same thing, Rad said, "What did your note say, Staci?"

I shook my head, avoiding his eyes.

"Nothing very interesting. Like Penelope, it just had some vague clues and riddles on it. If you want, I can bring it down to show you later after I go back to my room…"

Rad nodded, looking satisfied. I wondered again if he really didn't receive a letter, and if so: why not? Why would he lie to us if he did receive one?

Perhaps for the same reason I was lying now, I considered. There was no way I could show him my letter later, so I prayed he'd forget about my offer.

Was it possible that Rad's letter, or even Penelope's that she had dodged the answer to, said the same thing as mine?

I didn't reveal the contents of my letter because it read: *The Beechwood killer is here in the house.*

Chapter Twenty-One

Lolly

The sun had settled beyond the horizon, final shimmers of twilight catching in the leaves of the treetops, sending mini-sparkles across the pitch-black surface of the pool.

I'd given myself some time to consider it, and now my mind was made up.

I'd come here searching for answers; in my mind, I thought that the killer was still out there, and he was the one taunting me with those letters.

But if there was a killer on the loose in Rock Hill again, or he'd been here all along and just stayed dormant, then I needed to know about it. I needed to finish him off for good, before he tried to kill any more young people again. Like my daughter, only a few years younger than I was at the time of the murders…

But the longer I thought about it, the more convinced I became ... the killer probably would have struck again by now, after all these years.

The thought of him still being here was scary, but now there was something else to worry about—something equally unsettling. Someone here was trying to point the finger at me ... someone who knew too much about it.

The thought of someone trying to pin the murders on me after all these years, and being carted away to prison, leaving my daughter and dad to fend for themselves ... no, that was unacceptable.

I had to leave this place. No amount of money or truth was worth it. Coming here was a dangerous idea in the first place, and staying here after getting that bizarre letter was just plain dumb.

I considered going back inside to tell the others, but first, I wanted to alert the guards out front and Mary Beth that I was leaving the premises. If something went down tonight ... I wasn't going to stick around and get blamed for it. Or worse yet, chased again by another psycho.

I need to get out of here, the sooner the better.

Unsure if I would have to sign something before leaving, I got on my feet and headed for the narrow, twisty, dirt path that would lead me back to the front gates I came in.

As I walked, with the hush of trees whispering all around me and the eyes of critters watching in the dark, I thought about my daughter. Just to see her face and feel safe again back in our home ... that alone was priceless. *What possibly possessed me to come here in the first place?*

It was pitch-dark when the trees parted before me, revealing the long metal fence of the Beechwood estate, and the gates we'd come in through only hours earlier. As I approached, an uneasy hush fell over me—the gates were locked tight, as expected. But there were no guards on duty in sight.

Someone had locked us in here. Probably someone who had no plans to let us out, I thought, fearfully, heading down the path for the guesthouse to find our hostess, Mary Beth Penner.

Chapter Twenty-Two

Cornelius

As soon as I heard Staci's confession, I knew what I had to do. While the others kept talking and gathered in the sitting room by the old fireplace, I slipped away, excusing myself to go to the kitchen. But it wasn't the kitchen I was looking for; it was the room in the hallway behind it. The library.

It wasn't much of a library at all—a pitiful collection of twenty dog-eared paperbacks and several worn-out hardcovers collecting dust in a central alcove. I headed straight for the desk, trying to remember what I was supposed to do when I was ready to make my guess on the impostor.

When I saw the blank envelopes and slips of paper, it came back to me. I scribbled my name on the outside of the envelope, then wrote 'STACI' in all caps. Tucking my paper inside it, I licked the envelope and sealed it tight. *There. All done.*

It wasn't much of a guess, considering that Staci had all but confessed to coming in her roommate's place. *What a bitch!*

I waved the envelope in the air and did a full spin, eyeing the walls for cameras.

There didn't appear to be any.

I hope Staci's admission doesn't nullify my guess, I thought, feeling flickers of doubt. But that wouldn't be fair! Perhaps I could even sue the owner if they refused to pay my 500k, since there was nothing in the original letter at dinner that specified someone couldn't confess if they were indeed the impostor.

What if she isn't though, really? What if she made that up to get others to guess, just so she could make us guess early and give herself more chances at the money…? My heart pounded in my chest as I gripped the letter tightly, knuckles whitening.

I would feel like an absolute moron if that were the case, but then again … Staci didn't look smart enough to pull that off. She seemed like a stupid, naïve girl, to me. And her confession sounded pretty genuine. I thought back to their strange conversation in the hallway upstairs. *Who cares if that weird bitch Bonnie is Staci's mom? It probably isn't true anyway. Don't these morons realize that our real host is just fucking with us, playing some sort of game and creating confusion, as well as distractions…?*

"What am I supposed to do now?" I said, wandering around the room. But then the final step hit me. I needed to open the under-desk drawer and place my guess inside. *Duh. How could I forget?*

When I opened the drawer, I expected to find it empty. But there was an envelope inside it, and it was addressed to me. I took it out and slid my guess envelope in its place. The letter had short instructions:

Behind the books, you will find a tool. Take the tool to Staci's room and use it to pry the false door open in the wall. Your prize awaits you beyond that door.

They'd already given me a hint about the turret, and I knew where the false wall was. It was almost insulting that they'd gone above and beyond to make sure I knew where to go. Nevertheless, I let the insult roll off my shoulders, trying to focus on the extra 500 g's, in addition to my 166k for staying, that I was set to collect.

One by one, I pulled the books forward on the shelf, exposing the brick wall behind them. When I reached the sixth book, I saw a shiny flash of metal. Quickly, I shoved aside the other books around it. There was an ax on the wall, anchored with industrial hooks. I lifted it off the hooks and examined it, then frantically looked behind me to make sure no one else was coming.

Well, this is an interesting "tool", I thought warily.

Carefully, I tucked the letter in my pocket and slid the ax in the back waistband of my pants. It felt sharp and dangerous pressed against my skin, but I tucked my shirt down over it and made for the stairs.

There were voices floating through the dining hall and entering the kitchen as I moved quietly toward the staircase to Staci's room. I could hear her in there, still chatting with the others.

"It's not certain that you're the impostor," Bonnie was saying to Staci. "You said that the letter was addressed to your channel name, The Forgotten and the Lost, so technically that means you were probably both invited. So, not an impostor…"

I froze, mid-step, in the doorway of the dining hall.

"Maybe you're right," Staci said, and I wanted to walk in that room and smack her right across the face. *She'd better not be right*, I thought, angrily. *If so, you cost me 500k. Well, 600k actually, because that means my time here is over if I guessed incorrectly…*

As I turned down the hallway and breached the steps, no one called out for me or seemed to notice I was there.

Upstairs, I went to the end of the hallway and slipped inside Staci's room once again.

"Please be the impostor," I muttered, staring at Staci's belongings on the floor. *Please.*

As I stood in front of the false veneer stone section of the wall, I noticed, for the first time, a small gap between two fake stones.

I inserted the sharp blade of the ax in the crevice and grunted with exertion as I pried at the fake stones. It took several tries, my body filling with panic, fear, and excitement all at once, but finally, I was able to pull the edge of the wall open a couple of centimeters. I pried it open the rest of the way with the ax, and then my fingers, releasing the false door with a satisfying sucking sound. The door sounded like a small child, releasing a long-held breath.

I pulled the door the rest of the way open, stepping into the bitterly cold, round room that used to serve as a lookout for the estate. Impulsively, I pulled the door halfway closed behind me, then went straight over to the slitted windows to look out over the property.

"Jesus." The view was tremendous—a flowing expanse of leafy, mature trees, and the small smudge of mountains and hills far in the distance of Rock Hill.

Up here, I felt on top of the world, like a true soldier protecting his land.

I was so distracted that I almost didn't hear the shuffling sounds behind me.

"Hello?" I whipped around and saw the flash of eyes in the corner of the tower. Someone was there, crouching in the corner ... waiting for me in the dark.

Chapter Twenty-Three

Penelope

Despite the shoddy rooming arrangements, I was relieved to be back in my own space, with my notes and my own thoughts. Flipping my handheld notebook open, I stared at the five names written on the paper.

- Rad, the irresponsible and failed cop.
- Cornelius, the arrogant architect with a penchant for jacking off in inappropriate places.
- Bonnie, the psychic turned fraudster who abandoned her own child.
- Staci, the imitation true crime detective who lied to her viewers and was left behind as a baby by her own mother despite her earlier claims.
- Lolly, the sad single-mother with an arsenal of trauma bulging from her closet.

I felt sorry for a couple of them, but most of them I didn't. And I knew a lot more about them than I'd written in my notes so far. But I wouldn't let them know that ... and I definitely couldn't share what was in my personal letter. If they knew what my letter said, then they'd all be ready to kill me ... or throw me out of here, at the very least.

I paused writing. There it was again. A small thud and then a sucking noise, coming from down the hallway. *What the hell are my fellow houseguests up to now?*

I crept to the door of my room and pressed my ear against the rough-cut wood. I waited a few moments, but the sound didn't return.

"Ah!" A loud knock rang out by my ear, on the other side of the door, nearly sending me into cardiac arrest. I clutched my chest, remembering that I'd need to take my heart pill I brought with me later.

"Who is it?" I demanded, my voice shakier than I'd like it to be.

"It's me," came a voice on the other end. *Bonnie, the psychic fraudster and piss-poor mother. Great.*

"What do you want?"

"Uh ... sorry if I disturbed you. It's almost ten o'clock. Our hostess should be back soon, for snacks and drinks. Remember?" Bonnie said, her own voice shaky on the other side.

"Of course I remember. I'll be down when I'm ready."

"Fine," Bonnie said. I listened to her footsteps as she walked down the hallway, glad to be rid of her. Like all the others, she definitely couldn't be trusted.

Chapter Twenty-Four

Bonnie

Penelope Jewel was the worst, I thought, clenching my jaw in anger and moved toward the end of the hallway to Staci's room. Like Penelope's door, Staci's was closed too. I knocked, waited. Then I knocked some more. Finally, I pressed my hand to the door with my eyes closed. I could feel someone there on the other side of it—or so I thought—but if Staci were in there, she didn't want to talk to me.

Honestly, who could blame her?

Earlier, when I touched her on the sofa, I sensed right away that she was lying. And as I held my grip, I knew for certain who she really was. *My Cecilia.*

I'd tried not to stare at her, those chestnut eyes with the green flecks, but I couldn't help myself. She looked a little bit like me, but those eyes ... those were her father's eyes.

I knew that Staci was my biological daughter, even if she didn't want to admit it. Trying to pawn it off on her friend Jan was strange ... for a moment, I'd even wondered if Jan was a real person or if she'd simply made her up as a cover story at the last second.

She doesn't want me to know who she is, who she really is. Unless ... what if she doesn't even know that she was adopted?

I knew the state had taken Cecilia in after Marco died, and I knew that a small, beautiful child would probably get adopted quickly. But I had no idea that she'd been here all along ... right here, in Rock Hill. We were so close, yet so far apart...

I pressed my hand to Cecilia—Staci's—door one more time and tried to channel my own energy through it. If I could just get her to listen, let me in ... it wasn't too late for us to get to know each other, at least a little bit.

"What on earth are you doing?"

I was startled, turning to look at Staci as she floated toward me down the hall.

A million times I'd imagined this ... what she might look like after all these years. And now that the moment was real, it felt so out-of-body and overwhelming.

"I don't know," I said, seriously. Clearing my throat, I added, "We are all going downstairs to sit and wait for Mary Beth to return. Rad suggested I come up and tell everyone. But we're missing a couple..."

"Okay," Staci said, still tilting her head and watching me strangely. "I was downstairs, exploring a little more. This place is fascinating."

"It is," I said, relieved at the break in tension. I pointed a finger at her closed door. "Did you see the turret outside when we came in? It's sealed up, but it corresponds with the wall outside your room. Which means the original entrance to it was probably in your room, or nearby."

"Really?" Staci said, raising one eyebrow. That movement, all by itself, sucked the breath from my chest. I used to do it, too, when I was younger. Patronizing my mom or my gram, and they'd threaten: "Cock that brow one more time, young lady, and I'll pinch it right off your face."

"Yes, really," I smiled. "I grew up here, in Rock Hill. And I came back after ... well, anyway, I come from a long line of psychics and witches. And my great-gran used to tell me that towers and turrets are safe because they're round."

"How so?" Staci said. Her tone was flat, but I could feel a flicker of interest coming from her. I could offer her a chance to know more about her real family, her own bloodline ... if she'd only let me.

"Well, it's sort of silly, you see. Great-Gran used to say that turrets were made round so that the devil couldn't hide in any corners."

"I guess that makes sense," Staci said. She moved next to me—I could smell the spicy scent of her perfume or deodorant—and she turned the knob to her room.

"This place is kind of cool, I guess," she said, entering her room and leaving space for me to follow.

"Like these marks." Staci pointed at the west side of her wall. I stepped over the threshold and entered her room, glancing at the sleeping bags on the floor and her mauve overnight bag. *I want to know so many things about her ... how she grew up, what she was like, really like, and if she was happy...*

Perhaps if I asked about "Jan", she would tell me more about her...

"These. Come look." Staci was standing with her nose to the wall, studying a patch of scratches on the wall. There must have been dozens of them. They mostly looked like random scratches etched in the stone, but some of them formed letters. I noticed an 'M' and 'VV' in a couple of spots.

"Ah. I know what these are," I said, running my fingers over the markings. "Witches' marks."

"Witches' marks. That sounds creepy," Staci said, reaching out to touch the one that formed the letter 'M'. But she had a curious smile, and she didn't look creeped out. I remembered that she ran a YouTube channel, discussing cold cases of lost or murdered women. I couldn't wait to watch every single episode when I got back home.

"It's not creepy. Not really," I said. "Witches' marks were like protection spells. They were meant to keep the structure safe from dangerous people, or spirits."

"But what about the letters? Do you think these were their own initials they left behind?" Staci said.

I shook my head. "Probably not. Believe it or not, most witches weren't dark and evil like they're so often portrayed. Many times, their spells were made to invoke spiritual protection from figures like the 'Virgin of Mary'. That's probably what the M and the VV stand for. Virgins of Virgins..." I said, tracing the letters 'V'.

"Fascinating," Staci said. Her smile dropped and she stepped back from the wall and from me, as though she remembered the truth—that I was the felon mother who left her behind. The mother who couldn't protect her.

No spells to reverse time and correct my mistakes … I wish there were. Like the original Beechwood witches, my reputation and fate in regard to my daughter had been sealed long ago.

"When you see Jan, will you tell her about me? I know this sounds silly, but whenever I get the chance to wish on something—a candle or a falling star or number patterns—I always wish for her happiness, health, and safety. Always. There's nothing I want more than to see her thrive."

"I'll tell her," Staci mumbled, making for the door. "I'm heading downstairs to wait for our hostess. You coming?"

Chapter Twenty-Five

Rad

Lolly hadn't returned to the castle, and neither had our hostess, Mary Beth. As I paced back and forth in front of the windows, I couldn't help wondering if something bad was going on.

Why would someone write that macabre Lizzie Borden rhyme—with an even sicker twist to it—and leave it for Lolly, unless they suspected she was involved in her friends' murders all those years ago...?

I checked my watch again. It was almost ten o'clock. Mary Beth was supposed to return any minute; I'd expected her to show up early like she had before dinner—and I wanted to ask her questions when she came. Questions like, where was Lolly? And when will we get to find out who actually invited us here?

Also, there was a part of me also looking forward to the libations she had promised.

After what happened to the Reeks kid—what I did to him—I gave up drinking for a while. Over the years, I'd fallen on and off the wagon countless times. I was off of it when Kate died. I still couldn't get over it—that ridiculous cancer diagnosis. Here I was, the one who smoked and ate too much and drank till I couldn't stand up sometimes, and Kate barely touched the stuff ... she was healthy and good. She was everything I wasn't. It shouldn't have been her that died; god should have given the cancer to me. After all, I deserved it.

Since Kate's death, I'd stayed on the wagon. But tonight I needed a drink. One cold beer or one glass of Scotch wouldn't kill me. And if it did? Well, perhaps, that wouldn't be so bad either...

I just hoped Kate was holding a spot for me up there in heaven, negotiating with the dear lord to make an exception and let me in, despite my many faults and fatal flaws.

Voices echoed through the halls. One by one they came —Bonnie, Staci, Penelope.

"Where's Cornelius?" I asked them. He'd been aloof ever since Lolly's eruption in the hallway earlier.

"Well, that's what we were just coming to ask you," Penelope said, coming over and plopping in the wingback chair. She looked older in real life than she did on the back covers of her books, but she was pretty for her age. Too bad her personality was dreadful.

"What do you mean?"

"His name tag is gone from the front of his door. We peeked inside and his stuff was in there, but no Cornelius. And, like I said, no tag on the door anymore," Staci explained.

"You all stay here and wait for Mary Beth. Save me a drink if she brings me them. I'll go find Cornelius," I said.

While the others waited, I moved through the lower levels, clearing each room. Kitchen, dining room, bathroom, library. The books on the shelf looked shuffled around, but nothing else was out of the ordinary.

Finally, I went upstairs. If Cornelius wasn't up here, then I'd need to go through that creepy tunnel again and search for him outside. Perhaps I needed to go find Lolly, too. But she'd specifically asked me—no, told me—not to follow her.

All those years ago, when we got the call—that a scared and distraught teenager was two miles from here, picked up by a concerned citizen on the side of the highway—my partner and I arrived there to find Lolly Andrews. She was a tiny thing, birdlike and shivering; you could tell she had been through some sort of hideous trauma.

It took nearly an hour for my partner to get it out of her —I didn't have much luck, my patience too thin and my irritation rising with her by the second. That's when she told us about the castle. And about her three dead friends.

I wasn't sure if I believed her at first. Murders didn't happen in Rock Hill. But, of course, we came to the property. And just like tonight, we had moved from room to room … clearing each one, and then moving outside.

Eventually, we found all three bodies. Just like Lolly said we would.

The horror at the scene was so unbearable—for the first time in my life, I knew what that expression meant: 'I couldn't wrap my head around it'. Because that's exactly how it felt at the time—numbing and unreal and too big to be of this world.

Those kids' faces were barely recognizable, their bodies treated like meat, hack marks on their arms and legs. On their torsos and faces. And the one girl ... her neck cut almost all the way through.

A sick feeling rolled through my stomach, an omen ... that this night was leading up to something that was no good. Perhaps even worse than what happened all those years ago in the nineties...

"Cornelius?" I banged on his door once, twice. Then I let myself in.

Just like Penelope said, his stuff was here but he wasn't. I glanced at his open bag ... just clothes, pen, and paper. His sleeping bag was in the corner. Nothing of interest.

I moved to the next room, and then the next. Peeking my head in all the empty rooms, including my own. I even checked the extra upstairs bathroom. It was foul-smelling with a dilapidated pedestal sink and a ceramic toilet. But still no Cornelius.

Lastly, I checked Lolly's room.

I felt guilty going inside it, but I did it anyway. Lolly hated me, and I couldn't really blame her for it. Most days I hated me too.

I wasn't as soft or kind with Lolly as I should have been back then, barking questions and demanding answers. So caught up with focusing on the Reeks kid as a suspect that I gave up any opportunity to find the actual killer.

Even though Bobby Reeks was dead and there was never enough evidence to prove he participated in the murders, most of the townspeople still thought it was him. So, every time I saw his mother or father in town, at the grocery or the gas station, they gave me these awful looks. Not anger—I could handle that. No, they looked at me with pure, unadulterated sadness. Not only did I take their son away from them, but I'd tainted the entire family's reputation too. The looks they gave me told a story—that I'd ruined their lives after making a split-second mistake…

Lolly's sleeping bag was unrolled, spread out on the floor. Next to it was her bag. It was zipped up tight, but I squatted on my haunches and opened it anyway.

The drawings were right on top.

I drew in a breath as I took them out … there were eight of them in all, and they looked rather old.

I flipped through them, praying Lolly didn't return and punch my lights out for it.

But the more I looked, the more unsettled I became. Each of the drawings were dark, sort of haunting. A creepy stuffed bunny; a scared looking eyeball; a haunted girl who looked just like Lolly; girls standing in front of a castle-like structure…

The drawings were good but dark, but not *suspiciously* dark … all except the one.

I held it up, studying the image. A childlike castle in the distance; a girl with an X over her mouth; and most eerily, an ax beside the girl's head that looked like it was dripping blood.

Did Lolly make these drawings herself, or did she find them?

Perhaps drawing is her way of coping with the trauma now, even if the subject matter is eerie and strange, I considered.

But when I flipped the drawings over, I saw that her initials were on the bottom: L.A.

And they were also dated: March, April, and May of 1996.

She didn't create these drawings in response to her trauma; she created them *before*. Before the murders even took place…

How strange was it that a young girl was drawing pictures of an ax and a girl and a castle, mere months before her friends were murdered with an ax?!

Chapter Twenty-Six

~TEN O'CLOCK~

Staci

We started our night in this room only a few hours ago, but we started at six and now there were only four of us. Where was Lolly? Did she really decide to leave, without even taking her stuff? And where the hell was that creep, Cornelius?

Suddenly, I had an idea. "Maybe Cornelius went to the library and guessed who the impostor was. After all, he was there when I told everyone else about me keeping the invite for myself instead of Jan…"

"Are you saying he guessed it was you and then was forced to leave? If so, then that means he guessed wrong. And if he was wrong…then you were lying to us about being the impostor, after all," Penelope said, slyly. She was sitting in that wingback chair, arms crossed at her ankles, looking at me with disdain.

"I told the truth about that. If that makes me the impostor, then I am. But maybe not … I have no idea anymore. I'm just thinking aloud about what could have happened to Cornelius…"

Rad was coming back down the stairs, an anxious tic moving in his cheek. He looked positively sick, his face ghostly pale and his arms patchy with what looked like hives.

"Are you okay?" Bonnie asked him.

"Fine. I didn't find Cornelius either," Rad said, moving to the fireplace and resting his elbow on the hearth.

Minutes passed, and we all sat there in silence. Waiting.

"Where the hell is our hostess?" Penelope said, finally breaking the silence. "I need a glass of wine or something. And some snacks."

"She's probably just running behind. We should be gracious and patient," Bonnie said. But the way she was looking at Penelope Jewel didn't make her seem like a poster child for patience.

I opened my mouth, then closed it. I wanted to tell them what my note had said—that there was a killer in the house. But it seemed so ridiculous, and we had been brought here for a chance to win money—so wasn't it possible it was some sort of game to make me and the others paranoid?

I'd nearly forgotten already about my scrunchie and necklace, that I was recording. My whole purpose for coming here was to get content for my channel, and my viewers… I wanted to share what I learned with them. Not the other houseguests. So, perhaps, keeping what little info I had to myself was my best bet for now.

But nothing about this whole thing was going as planned.

I never could have anticipated this part … my mother. *My fucking mother.* Could it be the truth, or was Bonnie some sort of paid actor, meant to rile me up and think she was the one who left me all those years ago…?

She's not your mother, even if it's really her, I reminded myself.

For most of my young life, I had no idea that I'd even been adopted by Michael and Aubrey Churchill. I thought they were my mother and father. And I thought that Andrew was my real brother.

They waited until I was thirteen to tell me, and that was a big mistake.

Nothing felt the same after that. I questioned everything. I tried to search for my biological parents, with no luck. My adopted parents denied knowing anything about my real ones, only that my father was dead, and the state had taken me away from my mother. First, came the anger … then the depression. And not long after, the swings of mania, and the bipolar diagnosis and therapy.

I started to feel better after treatment. Started to forgive my adopted parents and move on from it … but then they died suddenly in a car accident, and I hated the world because of it. I fell so hard, I never thought I'd come out of that deep, black hole of depression.

All I had left in the world was my brother Andrew. I

loved him, but deep down, I knew he wasn't my real brother and that hurt too. *The way he looks at me sometimes … like he doesn't know or understand me. God, that hurts so much.*

"What does Jan like to do for fun?" Bonnie leaned in and asked me, her breath hot on my cheek.

"None of your damn business," I said, jerking out of my seat and walking over next to Rad. *She's relentless! I need to get away, and stay away, from Bonnie … or I might lose my shit in front of everyone.*

"I'm going to walk to the guesthouse and see what's keeping Mary Beth," I said, resolutely.

I expected some pushback from the former cop, but he looked relieved when I said it. "I'm going with you," he declared.

"I don't need a babysitter," I snapped.

"I know, but I want to look for Lolly," Rad said.

"Okay, fine."

I headed for the door with Rad by my side, not looking back once at my mother. It was my turn to leave her behind.

Chapter Twenty-Seven

Penelope

"And then there were three," I said, tapping my nails boredly on the arm of the sofa.

"There's only two of us here," Bonnie snapped, turning from her perch at the window to give me a look.

Surprised she heard me with all of her obsessive, mother-hen gawking, I said, "You forgot about the perv. Cornelius never left. He's too big, loud, and gawky to go anywhere quietly. No, he's still in here somewhere. Probably hiding in the shadows, watching us from the corner with his pants around his ankles and his dick in his hand."

"You're a vile woman," Bonnie said, not bothering to look at me this time.

"Indeed," I sighed. There once was a time when my dry humor was a hit at parties. My dark jokes used to go over well, at least in the days of my youth, or more precisely, in the days of my success. But eventually people figured out that I'm like this all the time. Cynical, sarcastic, cold. *Unpleasant to work with*, as my last editor said in an email. *Doesn't work well with others*, wrote the one before her.

I never said I was nice.

"Why are you just standing there? It's dark out. Can you even see Staci?"

"No, and I'm worried. We don't know who brought us here, exactly, and she could be in danger. I never should have let her go. Maybe I should go out there too..." Bonnie said, her expression softening as she looked at me.

I barked a laugh, and Bonnie flinched.

"It's a little too late to play mommy dearest, isn't it? What are you going to do—walk around like a helicopter parent, following a twenty-five-year-old around? You missed the boat on that one, lady. I hate to be the one to tell you..."

"Fuck you," Bonnie said, turning away.

"Tell me how you really feel, Bonnie. At least you're telling the truth for once in your life. No tricks or psychic gimmicks up your sleeve, just angry words this time," I said.

But she didn't take the bait this time or catch my reference to her shady past.

"I'm going to the kitchen to look for snacks," I said, excusing myself.

I stood, knees cracking, and made my way to the kitchen. As I cut through the dining room, cleared of our earlier meal and discussion, I couldn't help noticing how dark and gloomy the house had become. Now that it was nighttime, there was no natural light. Only sickly yellow bulbs in the corners, casting the corpse-like room with shadows. The kitchen wasn't much better, just a soft light over the ancient stove top—that didn't even look functioning—and a single fluorescent illuminating the hallway off the kitchen.

I wasn't really looking for snacks.

I entered the back hallway and slipped inside the library. If Cornelius really did make a guess at the impostor, there should be evidence of it in here.

"Bingo," I said, counting the tiny slips of paper and envelopes. Only one was missing.

I opened the drawer under the desk and there it was, a sealed envelope with Cornelius's name scribbled on it.

Tempted to tear it open and read his guess, I took the envelope out and held it up, trying to read through the stationery. But there wasn't enough to see through it.

I don't care about the money anyway, and knowing Cornelius, he impulsively ran in here and guessed Staci's name right after her confession upstairs.

I wasn't buying Staci's story for a minute. I knew that Jan was real; I'd seen her on their stupid detective wannabe channel. But Staci was hiding something more; I could feel it. I knew more about Staci than I'd like to … her background, adopted parents who tried to raise her, that she was riddled with mental health issues and "mommy issues". I rolled my eyes, thinking of Bonnie.

Returning the envelope to the drawer, I turned to leave but then I saw a small, folded piece of paper on the floor by the bookshelf, nearly concealed in the shadowy corner.

I scooped it up. Right away, I knew it belonged to Cornelius—a frantic attempt at a blueprint (who else but a failed architect would draw the castle like this?). He'd messily marked the rooms on the first and second floors, but his main point of interest was the turret; he'd circled it, retracing it several times. And there was a big X written on the small block that marked Staci's room.

"Damn. What did he find?" My curiosity was piqued.

I put the drawing in my pocket and quietly headed for the twisted staircase. I was only a few steps from Staci's door, when I heard the sound of footsteps coming up the stairs.

"Why are you going in my daughter's room?" Bonnie said, eyes flickering with anger as she came down the hall.

I made a whirring motion over my head. "Like I said, helicopter parent. Too late for that, my dear."

"Shut up," Bonnie said, stopping right next to me.

"Apparently our Peeping Tom was interested in something in Staci's room. I'm going to check it. Come with me if you must," I challenged.

Chapter Twenty-Eight

Bonnie

"I know exactly what he was looking for," I said. The makeshift map was in my hand; I clenched my jaw, heartbeat thumping in my ears. "The real question is: why?"

Penelope and I were standing in my daughter's assigned room, looking for whatever "X marks the spot" point that Cornelius had been seeking.

"Care to enlighten me then?" Penelope asked. She looked bored already, nudging my daughter's sleeping bags with her studded Louboutin flat.

"Not really," I muttered, running my hands over the stones until I found what was clearly veneer. It made sense —this area corresponded to the turret on the exterior wall of the castle. But why was Cornelius trying to get inside when our instructions clearly stated that it was sealed off, and against the rules to enter?

"It's the turret," I said, placing both hands on the veneer. A shiver ran through me, starting with the tips of my fingers and forging a path all the way down to my toes. I tried to recall my gran's words about the rounded architecture and protection of the turret's design, and I thought about the strange witches' marks on the wall. Despite my gran's stories, there was nothing good or protected about this turret. I could sense something dark and awful waiting on the other side.

"Just know that if we go inside, you'll probably be forfeiting your winnings. The instructions clearly stated that it was sealed off and we are supposed to follow the rules. I never cared much for rules myself and I don't need the money, but you … I'm guessing you need it bad…" Penelope said. She'd moved closer now, hands on her hips as she stared at the wall in defiance.

"Shut up and go get something we can use to bust through this false wall with," I said.

Expecting her to refuse, I was pleasantly surprised when Penelope simply nodded and left the room. While she was gone, I inspected Staci's bag. The zipper was undone, pieces of clothing bulging from the top of it.

Carefully, I bent down and dug my hand inside, reaching under the clothes. Like me, my daughter had a habit of burying things she wanted to hide.

I removed several papers—a set of instructions for operating a hidden camera, and some sort of listening device. *So, Staci broke the rules as well. She's trying to record this process, probably for her channel, even though she's not supposed to.* I felt a small glimmer of pride.

Underneath the instructions, I also found Staci's personal letter. I remembered what she'd said earlier, about hers containing clues. But I quickly learned that was a lie.

The Beechwood killer is here.

I gasped, then yelped, as Penelope fluttered back into the room. Promptly, I stuffed the papers back into my daughter's bag.

"Snooping through your daughter's stuff to make up for lost time?" Penelope snarked.

I was going to tell her to go fuck herself. But then I saw the hammer in her hand.

"Found this in the kitchen downstairs. There's candles and matches and a few screwdrivers too, in case we need them," Penelope said.

I waited for something snarky to follow, but nothing did.

"I'll do it." I reached for the hammer in her hand.

"I might be old but I'm strong," Penelope said, pulling back with the tool. I watched, adrenaline buzzing, as she went straight to the veneer wall and swung the hammer with more gusto than I would have thought possible at her age.

Moments later, she'd created a hole, and we were both pulling away at the fake stone siding to get inside.

"Stop!" I stepped back from the wall. "There's someone in there."

"Is it the perv? Let's peep on him, for a change," Penelope laughed, stepping up to the opening and sticking her whole head inside it.

She released a blood-curdling scream.

Chapter Twenty-Nine

Rad

"It's way too quiet out here," Staci said, sweeping the flashlight over the trees.

We were looking for Lolly Andrews along the tree line of the forest. But she was nowhere to be found...

There was a hush in the air, as though we were the only creatures—forest animals included—around for miles and miles...

And yet. There was an uneasy feeling growing inside me, as though we were being watched. There were no cameras inside the castle, at least none that could be seen with the naked eye. As far as I could tell, there were no cameras or listening devices outside; even those that were strategically placed in the trees or crumbling bird baths, would be spotted if you looked hard enough...

"Agreed. It's quiet," I said, my own voice sounding

strange and foreign in my ears. There was only one flashlight, so I'd given mine to Staci. If something happened and we got separated, she needed it more than me.

Despite our searching so far, we'd also found no signs of Lolly. No signs of anyone, in fact.

"Do you think the guards are taking a break?" Staci asked, stepping through a gap between two trees and walking straight ahead into the yawning mouth of the forest.

"I don't know."

When we'd approached the gate earlier, we found no trace of the guards. Plus, we were still locked inside.

My eyes traveled side to side over the forest, looking for movement ... shadows. But still, there was nothing.

That growing pit of fear was rising, spreading from my stomach to the rest of me. The property extended for nearly a mile eastward, and less than three-quarters of a mile away was the location where I'd recklessly shot Bobby Reeks. I didn't want to go back there; I needed to avoid that direction for my own sanity ... but how would we get out of here if the guards didn't return?

Surely, there was a gap somewhere ... or I'd just have to take the risk and try to climb over and grapple with the electric fencing...

Staci was still chattering; she seemed nervous, but more in control than I was feeling. The locked gates, the missing guards, everything we'd seen so far...

"Wait. Staci, I must warn you..."

Staci stopped in her tracks and turned toward me, shining the light right in my face.

"I don't know if it's safe to be out here. That's why I came with you. I don't think we should look for Lolly right now. I think we should go check in with Miss Penner. She might have more information for us, or she can tell us if she's spotted Lolly and when the guards are scheduled to return."

The guesthouse was back in the direction from which we'd come, and there were soft yellow lights blooming from inside the small building, beckoning us to come back from the shadowy tree line, to somewhere safer and better lit...

"What are you afraid of?" Staci moved closer to me, too close. She fingered the necklace at her throat.

"Look. I found some drawings in Lolly's room. They were ... disturbing to say the very least."

"So?" Staci inched in even closer, and I took a wide step back.

"So, they were dated from back then ... before the murders. And there was an ax in one of the drawings. I don't think she was involved back then, I really don't ... but anything is possible, yeah?"

Staci leaned her head side to side, considering. She looked ghoulish in the glow of the flashlight, and I could see a flash of worry in her eyes.

"The murderer is almost always male. You must know that, Rad."

"I do. But the killer was never found ... and I just don't

want to take any chances out here. I feel responsible for you, so I wanted to tell you about what I'd found."

"Thank you for telling me," Staci said. She hesitated, chewed her lip.

"What?" I pressed.

"I should share this with you, too. My letter didn't contain any random clue. It said that the Beechwood killer was here, here at the castle with us…"

"Jesus." I breathed in through my nose and out through my mouth. "Maybe it's just someone fucking with us … making a game out of our fears. Just because we didn't see any cameras doesn't mean there aren't any." But I was talking to the wind, and mostly trying to convince myself. My mind flashed back to Lolly's drawing, the one with the girl and the ax. Could they possibly mean something, that she was involved back then? Images of those kids' faces, slaughtered and left for dead, flashed like camera bulbs in my mind. And Bobby Reeks … his face, too. Although I was responsible for that death…

What was the likelihood of a young girl drawing gruesome pics with an ax, and then seeing her friends get murdered with one…? That was the part that was bothering me. I'd never suspected her involvement back then, but now…

"Let's go find Penner," Staci said, touching my elbow.

As we walked, Staci kept quiet and fell in step beside me. I stopped when we got close to the guesthouse. It was a small brick building with a couple of windows and a single entrance, and supposedly where our hired hostess was staying for the night. But why didn't she turn up on time to bring libations like she was supposed to? Had something happened to Lolly and that's what was causing our hostess to run late?

"It must be hard for you, being here," Staci said, her words like whispers in the dark.

"It is," I admitted, surprising myself as I stared ahead at the guesthouse. I saw two versions of it—the guesthouse, how it looked back then … and how it looked today. Mostly, it looked the same. Just older and more rundown.

"Didn't they find one of the bodies inside there? I wonder if our lovely host knows about that. She probably thinks it's better to be out here, instead of inside with us," Staci tsked.

"Yes. One of the boys' bodies was found inside. I'm the one who found it." Flashes of Thomas Tarton's wide open stare, his body splayed open for all to see. Those deep red gashes on his chest and arms…

I shuddered and blinked back the memories. All that trauma … it didn't feel like it really affected me back then, but nowadays, it came roiling back when I least expected it.

"Where were the others found?" Staci said, again moving in too close to stand next to me, as though she wanted to catch every word.

I suspected that she already knew these answers, being that she ran a YouTube channel that discussed true crimes just like this one.

"Monica Collins was found near the mouth of the

tunnel, and Mike Wilcox was found inside the turret," I told her.

Staci looked at me, assessing me, for several too-long seconds.

"I'll go up and knock. You can stay here," she offered.

"No. I got it," I huffed, marching up to the door and banging on the side with my fist.

When no one came, I knocked again, harder this time. Finally, Staci came over, stood on her tiptoes, and tried to peek through the window to get a look inside.

"See anything?"

"Wait." Staci darted over to the other window, cupping her hands around her face and pressing it up to the glass.

"Holy fuck. She's lying on the floor in there, Rad. I think Mary Beth might be dead…"

Chapter Thirty

~ELEVEN O'CLOCK~

Staci

R ad's face was sheet-white and sweating as he sprung into action, running around the outside of the guest building, looking for intruders.

Finally, he joined me back inside the guesthouse where I stood next to Mary Beth's crumpled form on the floor. Her eyes were wide, unseeing—but it looked as though she'd had the scare of her life.

"Her neck, it's cut so deeply…" I leaned forward to look, but my stomach twisted in on itself. I'd looked at crime scene photos and seen more gruesome things than I'd like to over the years, due to my true crime obsession. But seeing a corpse in real life was something else entirely.

"Step back from there. This is a crime scene," Rad warned me, his voice stern and so much louder than usual.

"Do you think this is some sort of twisted game? Like a

murder mystery, and this isn't real ... or something?" I said, hopefully. But deep down, I knew that wasn't the case.

"I've seen enough dead bodies to know when one is real," Rad said, sharply. He stopped, staring down at Mary Beth as though he were seeing someone else in her place.

"Maybe she brought a cell phone with her. Let's search for it," I suggested, looking around the tiny one-room guesthouse.

Unlike our assigned rooms, Mary Beth's contained a cot and comforter.. There was a compact table with a few bags of sealed snacks and toiletries inside it. In the corner, there was also a refrigerator, probably to house our libations she was supposed to bring over at ten.

"You see a purse anywhere?" I said, carefully stepping around Mary Beth's body and moving closer to Rad. Earlier, I'd been trying to get close enough to record our conversation for my viewers, but now, this all felt otherworldly ... and thoughts of my own plans subsided.

If there's a killer out here, then I might not ever make it back home to my viewers...

"No, I don't see one." Rad moved around the small room, using the edge of his shirt to open the few cabinets and drawers that lined the edge of the guesthouse. "There's nothing in here at all. Wait. No, just a set of pajamas and spare undergarments," Rad sighed, looking in the final drawer.

"No cell phone. No guards. And the gates are locked tight. We need to find a way to call for help..." I was in shock, I supposed, because none of this felt real at all. I glanced one last time at Mary Beth's body on the ground.

"Someone cut her. It looks like … it looks…"

"Like someone got her with an ax," Rad finished. "Try not to look, Staci. Come on. We need to get inside the main house and find the others, and then we need to lock ourselves inside and wait until someone comes in the morning, or hopefully sooner to relieve us. The longer we stand here, the more we are contaminating things and putting ourselves at risk. Whoever did this might come back … we need to warn the others and find a way to break through that fence or look for an alternative way out. Now!"

Right on cue, we heard the sounds of high-pitched screaming. They were coming from inside the castle.

Chapter Thirty-One

Penelope

"We're up here!" I shouted, listening to the shouts and heavy foot thumps of Rad and Staci returning. Rad burst into the room like a wild bull; Staci followed in his footsteps.

Bonnie was still bent over in the corner, wiping vomit from her lips.

"Don't look. He's dead," Bonnie warned them, looking young and sheepish crouched like that on the floor. I was still standing in the broken-in entrance to the turret, shocked and confused by what my eyes were seeing. Cornelius's limp, dead body lay inside. Someone had hacked him up with an ax, his face butchered like a slab of beef. He was sprawled out on his back, mouth open wide in horror, as though he'd looked the killer right in the face before he died.

The murder weapon—a large ax with a wooden handle —was lying on the stone floor beside him, coated in congealing hunks of blood and meat.

Rad nearly knocked me aside to get a closer look, and Staci moved beside him to see the body too. Strangely, she seemed unfazed by it, her eyes blank. Lost…

"We need to get out of here. Now. Let's move down the hallway to a safer room," Rad ordered.

"How did this happen…? Why?" Staci said, glancing over at her biological mother in the corner.

"We found a paper Cornelius left behind. Some sort of hand-drawn map. He was looking for this sealed off entrance to the turret. I guess someone was waiting for him inside. I don't know…" I told her.

"My room… oh my…" Staci looked around her own room, as though seeing it for the first time.

"Now!" Rad barked, again. He was already standing by the bedroom door.

"He's right. Let's get out of this room," Bonnie said, standing up on shaky legs and swiping at her mouth and shirt to remove the evidence of her violent sickness earlier.

"Okay. But one of y'all better not be the killer," I huffed. One by one, Rad led the four of us through the hallway and down to his bedroom.

"My room has a window facing the front. We can listen and watch for intruders. And lock ourselves in until morning," he said.

I considered arguing with the man, but I didn't have the energy. This whole evening was turning out to be way more fucked up than I ever could have imagined.

As soon as we were all in Rad's bedroom, he locked the door behind him and started walking around the perimeter of the room, feeling all along the walls for more hidden alcoves or rooms.

"We can't wait until morning. We need to get out of here now!" Staci pleaded.

"She has a point. Why stick around? There's an ax back there with…" Bonnie said.

My stomach churned as I imagined the red, raw meat left of Cornelius's face.

"She's right" Staci said, glancing at her mother. "What if we tried to use that ax to get through the fence? All we need is a small enough gap to climb through…"

Rad's attention was still focused on the perimeter; he moved all along the wall, pressing his hands against it.

"I don't think there's anything else on the other side of this wall," I said, pointing a thumb at the eastside of the room. "The turret connected to Staci's room, but yours is just brick and stone on the other side of this…"

Rad looked at me, then nodded. "Listen. I'm not saying we can't attempt to escape. The ax might work … but for now, we need to be cautious. The killer is close and it's dark out there. We need to be smart about this, stick together."

Rad stopped what he was doing, rubbing his hands warily through his hair and over his jowls. "Did either of you go outside earlier?" he asked, pointing first at me and then to Bonnie.

I shook my head. "No, we've been together this whole time." Mostly.

"Why do you ask?" I pressed.

The ex-cop was hiding something … but what?

Staci cleared her throat. "Because Mary Beth is dead, too. We found her in the guesthouse outside. It also looks like someone killed her with an ax or a sharp weapon…which means there could be more weapons and he's probably still out there, or inside. Close by."

I gasped. "What about the guards? Why can't they let us out? Didn't you alert them?"

Rad shook his head. "No sign of the guards when we were out there, and the gate is locked. We're stuck here for a while, at least until it's safe to try to get away."

Well, this was a plot twist I didn't see coming.

"And Lolly? Did you find her?" Bonnie said, her voice quiet as she moved to the small, barred window, looking out over the property.

"No sign of her," Staci said.

"Well, the way I see it," I said, pacing the room, "most of us are accounted for. Or dead,," I said, nodding back in the direction of Staci's room and the turret. "Only one person is missing, and that's pretty suspect, don't you think?"

Lolly.

None of us had to say her name, but we were all thinking the same thing … where could she be, and what was she capable of?

Chapter Thirty-Two

Bonnie

While Rad and Penelope argued over Lolly's capabilities and motives for murder, I went over to check on Staci.

"You okay? That must have been scary … walking into the guesthouse and finding her, like that…"

"I'm fine," Staci said. There was still a sharpness to her, but I felt a softening too. I wanted to reach out and hug her, burrow her in my arms like I did when she was a baby.

"I know this isn't the time," I started, but Staci lifted a hand to stop me.

"Like I told you earlier, I have a mom. Had one. And a dad. They died many years ago in a car accident. You're not my mother, Bonnie," Staci said, looking me long in the eyes and making herself very clear.

"I'm so sorry about your parents, Staci. I really am."

There was an ache in my chest; not only did she lose her biological parents at an early age, but then she lost the ones who raised her as their own. *Oh, my poor girl. My poor, sweet girl.*

"Thank you," Staci said, tiredly.

"I won't bother you about this anymore. Just please tell Jan I'm sorry, okay? Tell her that I've missed her every single day of my life since I lost her, and I will miss her every day from here until the end of time…"

Staci squeezed her eyes shut. "Will do," she said, finally, refusing to look my way.

I moved away from her, giving her space, and walked closer to Rad and Penelope.

"I think we can all agree that the impostor isn't Staci after she explained herself earlier. Yes, Jan was possibly invited too, but that doesn't mean Staci wasn't included," I said.

"What's your point?" Penelope snapped, giving me a sharp look.

"Well, if we can figure out who the real impostor is or was … then I think we'll know who the killer is too. The impostor and the killer are probably one and the same, don't you all agree?" I looked over my shoulder at Staci, but she was staring at the floor by her feet.

"Make sense," Penelope shrugged.

"No," Rad said, his voice firm.

I gave him a questioning look. "Why not?"

"I know that the killer isn't one and the same," Rad said, "because I'm the real impostor."

Chapter Thirty-Three

Rad

"When I heard the news about the new owner and the announcement about guests being invited to the castle, I called in some favors from a few old friends," I said, looking around the room at the ladies' shocked faces.

"I'm surprised you have any friends in this town," Penelope quipped. The woman was insufferable, but I was starting to get used to her nasty humor.

"Not many friends, that's true," I admitted. "But I reached out to a few people, and we were able to trace the PO box to an LLC whose main office was an empty storefront in Massachusetts."

"I don't understand," Staci said. "Are you telling me there is no real owner, just some straw company with the Beechwood LLC name that bought it? Why would an empty business in Massachusetts want anything to do with this tainted old place?"

I shrugged. "I have no idea. That's why I decided to come. To pretend to be one of the six ... I researched online how to draft up my own NDAs and fake documents, just in case I was questioned on my way inside by other guests, or our host. I even took my documents to a lawyer friend of mine to make sure he couldn't tell they were fictitious. Kept waiting for someone to stop me, to ask me what I was doing here ... but nobody did."

"How did you know about the NDAs if you never got an invitation, Rad?" I asked, narrowing my eyes in suspicion. The more these people talked, the less I trusted a single one of them.

"Well, not all of you were tight-lipped about getting invited. Staci flashed her invitation right on the screen during one of her videos when she shared the news that she was one of the six with her viewers. I simply zoomed in and copied down as many details as I could."

"But why?" Bonnie asked.

"I needed to know who was behind this. It didn't sound right to me. If it was a documentary or reality TV show, then we would have had major networks and producers down here, preparing to film it all. It was too hush hush to be legit. Now that I'm here, I still don't know what's going on, exactly. I think someone lured us out here...

"When I got here, I expected to find seven of us since I was an extra. But there were still only six which didn't make sense at first, but now it does. Staci's co-host was supposed to come with her too. I saw her name on the door when I came upstairs … three letters in her name, Jan. I used a marker to quickly change it to my name. None of you even seemed to notice," I said.

"Sneaky bastard," Penelope said, watching me shrewdly.

I shrugged, again. "I came to see who was behind this. I don't know their name, but I do know who they are now. It's the killer. And he's back after all these years…"

Chapter Thirty-Four

~MIDNIGHT~

Staci

We spent the next thirty minutes waiting in silence. The temperature had dropped significantly; I shivered uncontrollably from my seat on the floor in Rad's bedroom, wishing I was anywhere but here. It was going to be a long, scary night...if I even survived it.

Bonnie and Penelope sat on Rad's unrolled sleeping bag, and Rad himself stood guard at the window, watching silently for a killer.

Rad's proclamation made sense—who else would bring us back here and commit more murders, but the killer himself (or herself)? But, I'd spent enough time researching true crime cases to know ... killers like that rarely went underground, or dormant. They merely moved their location, or they died, and that's how they were finally stopped. There was no way the killer was here all along, never committing another murder for almost thirty years...

Rock Hill hadn't seen a murder in decades. Some people still liked to blame Bobby Reeks and his poor family for the murders in 1996. It was easier and more palatable to accept that theory; after all, it allowed the townspeople to rest easy, knowing he was dead and gone, justice served in some sort of half-assed way for what happened to those kids. And that there was no longer a killer on the loose...

But most people know that theory is bullshit. Most of us believe the real killer was never caught. That he had moved on to another city or small town ... or hopefully, that he'd died, ridding this earth from his evil...

Thinking back on other true crime cases in which a killer seemed "dormant" but wasn't, I recalled a third option: incarceration.

Perhaps the killer had been locked up all this time, and now they were back out in society. Walking among us...

I glanced over at Bonnie, supposedly my biological mother, and I considered her for the first time. What did I really know about this woman? Sure, she seemed apologetic and regretful. Sure, she seemed kind, albeit a little eccentric. But what if she was dangerous...? She would have been around the same age as Lolly and the other victims back then ... and she lived in Rock Hill, mere miles away, when the murders took place.

And Rad. He seemed nice enough, and protective. But, he'd been a drunk back in the day, supposedly, and he'd accidentally killed Bobby Reeks. He was around these woods back then, and he was here now. What if he killed Reeks to silence him for something? What if Officer Rad Williams was a bad dude back then, and he was still a bad guy now?!

Next, I glanced at Penelope. She was the oldest of our group, sure. But she was also the meanest. She seemed cold and hateful at times, and I'd heard that she was a real pain in the ass on the literary scene back in the day. She hadn't produced any new books in a while, and I wondered why. What had she been working on lately? Like the others, she was also from Rock Hill and could have been around at the time of the murders. She travelled a lot for her writing work, at least she used to. Going on book tours, perhaps committing other murders in random cities along the way…

My head was hurting as I tried to consider who could possibly be responsible for this. Who was evil enough to maim and murder Cornelius and Mary Beth that way…?

Lolly. She was the obvious suspect, and the only one missing from our group … well, those of us who were still alive. But could a thirteen-year-old really be capable of crimes that heinous back then? I didn't think so, but it wouldn't be the first time in history that a young girl did something atrocious to her friends.

All I knew was that I didn't trust a single one of them.

"I'm thirsty and I need to pee," I announced, breaking our group's uncommitted vow of silence.

"Me too," said Bonnie, eyes meeting mine.

I rolled my eyes. Was she just saying that to add support, or did she really need to go, I wondered, irritably.

"I'd kill for a drink right now myself," Penelope said, rubbing her cheeks with her neatly manicured hands. "Well, not kill," she said, looking up at the rest of us, "but you know what I mean. Y'all didn't happen to grab any of those drinks when you found Mary Beth...?"

We all looked at Penelope with shock and disgust. She truly was a vile lady.

"I need to pee," I repeated.

We all turned our heads to our overweight, fearless, macho leader, waiting for his approval.

I thoroughly expected Rad to refuse us (although I didn't plan to listen, even if he did), but he simply nodded.

"I need to use the bathroom too, and I think we should gather up things along the way that we could potentially use as weapons. Right now we're sitting ducks in here. I think it's a good idea that we're sticking together and locked in a room on high ground, but if the killer breaks down the door ... well..." He put up his hands and glanced back toward the window.

"We all go. But we stick together," Penelope said, looking serious and worried for the first time since arriving at the castle.

Rad led the way, opening the door to his bedroom an inch and looking down the hallway to make sure it was clear. He went first and I followed behind him, Penelope and Bonnie bringing up the rear. One by one, we went down the twisty stone staircase, and moved slowly toward the kitchen.

"I'll stand guard," Rad said, pointing toward the hallway off the kitchen that led to the central bathroom.

"If you insist," I said, rolling my eyes.

He made sure no one was hiding in there, and then I went inside. I used the toilet, washed my hands, and stared at my own reflection. Earlier, I'd stood right here, full of hope and eagerness to record this event for my viewers. Now, none of that seemed important.

After me, it was Penelope and Bonnie's turn in the bathroom, and finally Rad's, although I thought he might refuse to go.

"It's okay. I've got this," Bonnie said, holding up a sturdy brass candlestick she'd swiped from the front room as we were walking by. "If someone tries to get us while you're pissing, I'll knock them over the head with it."

Once Rad had finished his business, we all gathered in the kitchen.

"Drawers. Search quickly and grab anything that looks like it could potentially be used as a weapon. Like this," Rad said, holding up what looked like a heavy pipe wrench he found under the sink. He handed it to Penelope.

I dug around, looking for what I could use. Hopefully, something better than a wrench or candle holder…

"Guys … you need to come in here." It was Penelope's voice in the doorway of the kitchen. I hadn't realized she'd migrated so far away after taking her wrench. She was pointing a shaky finger toward the dining area we'd passed through earlier. "Was that note there on the table earlier, or did someone just put it there?"

I walked toward the table, my breath stuck like taffy in my chest, and picked up the envelope in the middle of the table. It was new. Anyone could have placed it there … hell, someone might have done it much earlier while the ladies were upstairs finding Cornelius, and Rad and I were out at the guesthouse with poor Mary Beth's corpse.

I lifted the letter. "It's addressed to the four of us," I said, holding it up for the others to see.

Chapter Thirty-Five

Penelope

"Let me read it," I said, taking the letter gently from Staci's hands. The girl looked positively spooked. Earlier, after coming in from finding the body, she'd seemed okay—perhaps, in shock—but reality was setting in now, and she looked downright terrified.

I ripped it open, removed the single-page letter inside, and turned toward the other to read:

"One of you is fond of stories. That must be me," I said, with a tight grin.

"Another likes to create her own. That's you," I said, sticking out my pointer finger at Staci as I held the letter.

"One of you wants to be hero but will always be the villain of this town. I don't think I need to say who that is," I said, avoiding Rad's glare.

"Lastly, one of you is a killer, masquerading as a teller of truth. You're the only fraud in the room," I said, pointing an accusatory finger at Bonnie.

"Let me see that!" Bonnie said, snatching the letter from my hands. The others gathered round, reading it for themselves:

> One of you is fond of stories
> Another likes to create her own
> One of you wants to be a hero but will always be
>   the villain of this town
> Lastly, one of you is a killer, masquerading as a
>   teller of truth

"Someone wants us to think you're a killer, Bonnie," I said, staring pointedly at the psychic.

"Maybe it's true. Maybe you did do it. Not only is my mother a felon and a deserter, but she's a killer too," Staci said, arms crossed tightly over her chest.

Chapter Thirty-Six

Bonnie

"This is madness! I've never hurt a soul in my life," I growled at Penelope.

"I'm pretty sure you were close in age to the other victims. Maybe you were here that night back in 1996, too, huh? They were making fun of you, so you tried to chop them up into bits!" Penelope accused.

"That's bullshit and you know it. They were all a few years younger than me. Yes, I came to the castle, just like most teens around here did. For drinking or screwing off, but I never knew those kids! I was working and on my way out of this town by that point…"

Penelope stared back at me, looking delighted by my anger, and I wanted nothing more in that moment than to wipe the smug look off her face.

"You have to believe me, Staci. You can trust me, I swear." But when I turned to look for my daughter, she was standing in the hall, her face a hard mask, and there was a knife clutched tightly in her fist.

Chapter Thirty-Seven

Rad

S taci held the knife in her hand, stretched out in front of her, fingers wobbly and unsure.

"Put down the knife now, honey. What are you doing?" Bonnie pleaded.

"I'm not your honey! And I'm walking out of here. Don't any of you try to stop me!" Staci warned, swinging the knife side to side, to show she meant it for our entire circle.

"Where did you get that?" I asked, taking a few small steps toward her. She was mostly focusing her rage on her mother, so I tried to back out of the group, and come up from beside her, finding a blind spot.

"I got it in the kitchen while we were gathering weapons, where else? I'm not a psycho like you. Or whichever one of you is hacking up people with an ax!" Staci screamed.

"Penelope and I were inside the whole time that you and Rad were out there searching … we obviously had nothing to do with Miss Penner's death," Bonnie said.

The arguments continued, and I took the opportunity to step closer to Staci. Just as I reached out to grab her hand with the knife, she whipped around to face me.

"Don't touch me!" she shouted, then she sliced my arm wide open with the blade.

Chapter Thirty-Eight

~ONE O'CLOCK~

Staci

The next thing I knew, I was running blindly through the dark. First, I headed toward my assigned bedroom, but then I realized that it wasn't safe on the second floor either, so I turned down the long east hallway and headed down the tunnel to go outside.

There were no lights in the tunnel, and I was about to turn around when I heard my mother behind me, shouting.

"Wait, Staci! Don't go off on your own! It's not safe!" Bonnie shouted.

Fuck off, I thought, quickening my pace and using my hands to feel along the wall and guide me. The walls of the tunnel were cold, damp, and scary, but within minutes, I could see a shimmer of light up ahead.

Bonnie still shouted behind me, but no matter now. I still

had the knife, and I was almost outside, the moon casting a welcoming glow up ahead.

Cutting the cop was stupid and impulsive, but I didn't trust him either. One of them was a killer, and the farther I got away from the group, the safer I would be.

There has to be a way out of here, even if the gates are locked … perhaps through the trees, along the fence's edge line, I could find an opening of some sort.

I didn't care about the money anymore, or about the views for my channel. I just didn't want to become like the girls I researched every night—the girls lost and forgotten every single day in this world.

Please just let me make it out of here alive.

The tunnel widened, the opening just up ahead. I burst through it, hit with a blast of cold November air … so crisp and chilling, I could have cried. I could see the stone garden ahead, and that hellish black pool … but Bonnie's voice still rang out behind me. *Go away, Mom.*

"Please!" Bonnie shouted behind me. I looked back, but I couldn't see her coming through the opening yet.

I stopped running and took a deep breath, and that's when I saw the dark shape of someone standing near the hedges. Before I could start running again, the figure stormed straight at me. They shoved me face first into the pool.

Chapter Thirty-Nine

Lolly

I waited until Staci could no longer hold her breath, and I squatted down as her head popped up from the deep, black water of the pool. Staci gasped for air, arms pinwheeling as she struggled to find something to grip onto at the water's edge.

"Get out of the pool," I said, pressing the muzzle of my gun close to her cold, wet cheek.

Chapter Forty

Penelope

U sing the raggedy towels I'd found in the bathroom, I made my best attempt at making a tourniquet for Rad's arm.

"It's fine," he complained, wincing as I pulled it tighter.

"It's not fine. I see why they call her Stabby Staci now! What a psycho! You're definitely going to need some stiches, if and when we get out of this hellhole," I said. "The wound needs cleaning. These towels look old and funky; let's hope you don't get tetanus. Or staph…"

"Thanks for all the encouragement," Rad said, still gritting his teeth. "I need to go after them. The killer is still out there, and I don't believe for a minute that it's actually Bonnie or Staci. Do you?"

"Who knows?" I sighed, tossing the leftover blood-spattered towels aside. We were sitting at the dining room table; I leaned my head against the back of the chair and closed my eyes. I felt so old and tired. So weary.

I usually go to bed at ten o'clock, snuggled in close with Robert.

"I'm going to check on them," Rad said, pushing back his chair and wincing again as he momentarily forgot about the deep, swelling cut on his arm.

"If you go after them, then you'll have to leave me behind," I said, pursing my lips.

"I get the feeling you can hold your own."

"Maybe so, but I do have a confession of my own to make."

Rad's eyebrows shot up. "Okay. Spill it."

"My note mentioned being surrounded by my research subjects."

"Research subjects?"

"You," I said, evenly. "I researched you, thoroughly, many moons ago. The failed investigation. The shooting of Bobby Reeks. The wrongful death suits the family filed but lost against the Rock Hill police department."

Rad adjusted his injured arm in his hand, but his face gave nothing away.

"Don't worry. That story never panned out. My editors hated it. They thought the story wasn't big enough, or good enough for public consumption."

"Can't say I'm disappointed," Rad said. He didn't look angry, just weary.

"But you weren't the only one. I also researched Bonnie. That whole fraud investigation, and the group she ran around with before she got busted; it was like a huge network of scammers. But, again, my publishers weren't interested in that kind of true crime story. Only blood and guts, the white-collar stuff just doesn't jive. Doesn't raise the heckles enough, you know?"

Rad shook his head. Maybe he didn't know.

"I also researched some of the others. Cornelius the perv, Lolly's possible role in the massacre…"

"And Staci?"

I sighed. "I was recently working on a piece about the dangers of armchair detectives, taking over the world with their biased news stories, and viral click-bait headlines," I said, bitterly.

"Let me guess. No one was interested in that one either," Rad said, sarcastically.

"Nope. But my point is … whoever's doing this seems to know a lot about us personally. Bonnie's past, Staci's adoption…"

Screams rang out, echoing from somewhere down in the hallway that led to the tunnel.

Rad jumped to his feet.

"I'll be back," he said, running straight toward the arguing voices.

I couldn't swear to it, but I thought I could hear Lolly Andrews out there…

Chapter Forty-One

Bonnie

T he moment I heard Staci's body hit the water, I stopped moving. Was the killer outside? Did she jump in the water to hide, I wondered.

But as I stepped quietly into the moonlight, I saw a different scene unfolding.

"Get out of the pool," Lolly said, sticking a gun against my daughter's face.

I felt the world fall out from under me. *Please, God, don't let my daughter die. Let it be me instead. She doesn't deserve this...*

Breathless, I watched my daughter emerge, pulling herself up from the side of the pool. She moved away from it; the whole time Lolly kept the gun aimed straight at her.

"Please." I stepped out of the shadows and into the

light, reflections in the pool dancing like wild demons. "Don't hurt Staci. You can kill me instead."

Staci turned to look at me, eyes wild and scared, but mostly she looked confused. After all she'd been through, she still tried to expect the best in others ... oh, how that hurt my heart.

Lolly frowned and turned the gun toward me. "Don't worry, Bonnie. I don't have to choose. I'll kill you if I have to."

Chapter Forty-Two

Rad

Before I became a cop, I was an impulsive man. My dad and granddad were police, my uncles and brothers firefighters. Our family events were always filled with reckless abandon—racing motorbikes, setting off fireworks, shooting guns, flipping off the backs of trampolines, four-wheeling in the dirt, doing wheelies while our mothers shouted for us to stop.

Impulsivity was like a family tradition. In my youth and early adulthood, it got me into more than my fair share of trouble. Even now, knobby knees and more than a decade retired, I find myself barreling through the tunnel, heading straight toward the danger, whatever that danger might be.

There were no lights in the tunnels, and I'd left my flashlight behind with Penelope ... so I stumbled through the darkness, reaching for the walls on either side of me, becoming disoriented. For a moment, I almost thought I was turned around, heading back inside instead of outside the castle.

Finally, a small bit of light up ahead. I could hear Lolly's voice—she was alive! She was threatening to shoot Bonnie and Staci. How the fuck did she get a gun? We were checked on the way in…!

I could hear the ladies coming toward me—was Lolly forcing them into the tunnel, back inside the house?

I was about to shout, to tell Lolly to stop right there, when I heard the sound of footsteps beside me.

I turned, pressed my back to the wall, held my breath, and listened.

There was nothing except the women coming through the tunnel, heading toward me … but then, there it was again, a small shuffle. Someone standing close in the dark.

Blinking, I looked around wildly, trying to get my eyes to adjust. But all I saw was blackness.

I didn't see the ax, but I heard it … the whoosh of the blade cutting through air. And then deep dark red, and the pounding of my own heart … until the ground rose up and slammed me right in the face.

Chapter Forty-Three

~ONE THIRTY~

Staci

We marched through the tunnel, Bonnie and I, Lolly behind us with the gun. I definitely underestimated her—I'd assumed she was dead or on her way home by now. Instead, she was waiting for a chance to kill us.

"Did you hear something?" Bonnie said, her breath stale beside me.

"Stop." Lolly must have heard something too. She nudged us to the side of the tunnel and turned up the brightness on her flashlight, shining it down the long passageway.

"What the hell is that?" I gasped, clutching Bonnie's arm for support.

"Hello?" Lolly, forgetting about us momentarily, walked forward with the gun in one hand and her flashlight in the other. For the first time, I had to wonder—where the hell did the gun come from? Did she sneak inside somehow, evading the guards when we arrived?

Suddenly, there was a skid of feet in the hallway, and the slap of someone running.

"What the hell?" Bonnie said, gripping me just as tightly as I was gripping her.

"Oh no," Lolly gasped. Further up the tunnel, I could see her bent at the knees, staring at the lump silhouette on the floor of the tunnel. That strange shape … that's what had confused my vision only moments earlier.

"It's Rad!" Lolly shouted.

Bonnie and I looked at each other. We could turn and run the other way, back out by the pool … away from Lolly and the gun. But instead we both ran toward her to offer help. We found her hunched over Rad, who was lying, crooked and strange on the stone floor. Blood pooled around his mouth, a halo of it forming around his head.

"It wasn't me," I said, dumbly, looking at Bonnie, then at Lolly.

"He's dead," Lolly said. "And his killer went that way, I'm pretty sure." She pointed her light down the long hallway, back toward the house.

"Well, let's not go that way then," Bonnie said, her voice ragged and pained.

"The killer used an ax again, even though we saw one upstairs. Maybe he has more than one," I muttered, head spinning as I looked down at the wound on Rad's neck. Someone had whacked at it so many times, I could practically see all the way through where his neck should be.

My stomach, finally reacting to it all, heaved and turned and puked away from the others, grunting.

I felt Bonnie's hand on my lower back.

"Don't," I snarled, wiping phlegm and vomit from my lips.

"Who did this? I thought I heard footsteps ... but it easily could have been one of you. You both came through here before ... maybe it was both of you, working together." Lolly's eyes flared, black and big as saucers in the glow of her handheld light.

"We didn't do anything," I said, glancing at the wobbly gun in her hand. "Someone killed Cornelius, and Mary Beth."

Lolly lowered her flashlight, and then the gun. "I know about Mary Beth. I found her dead in the guest house, and that's why I hid."

"Hid where, exactly?" I asked.

"Wouldn't you like to know," Lolly said, narrowing her eyes at me. "Who killed Cornelius?"

"We don't know. We've all been trying to huddle together and stay safe. Meanwhile you've been out here in the dark, running around or hiding ... doing God knows what," Bonnie snapped.

I reached over and squeezed her arm, a warning and a reminder: that Lolly had a gun. She was the one in charge here, at least for now.

"And now he's dead," Lolly said, pointing the gun in

Rad's direction. "Coming here was a huge mistake," she said, closing her eyes and letting out a long, heaving breath.

"Understatement of the year," I mumbled.

Lolly pointed the gun back at me. "We are going inside and I'm keeping an eye on all of you until the sun comes up and the police can be brought out to arrest whichever one of you did this. Or…" She looked out toward the end of the tunnel again, and I could almost hear her thoughts, as though she had spoken to them aloud: *unless the killer is someone we don't know … someone out there waiting to kill whoever is next on his list … perhaps, the same psycho from before…*

"Where's Penelope? Is she dead, too?" Lolly asked.

Right on cue, a woman screamed. Penelope was shouting for help.

Chapter Forty-Four

Lolly

Penelope was waiting at the mouth of the hallway, her hand clutched to her chest.

"I'm sorry, I was just so scared … waiting here by myself. Rad never came back," she said, looking sheepish. When she saw me emerge from behind Bonnie and Staci, her mouth fell open in surprise.

"Back from the dead. Again," she quipped, but then she saw the gun in my hand.

"What the hell is going on here?" She looked back and forth between Bonnie and Staci.

"Rad's dead," Bonnie said.

Penelope's eyes grew wider, and once again, she looked toward me and the gun.

"No, I didn't shoot him. Someone got him with an ax," I said.

Before she could say any more, I motioned toward the sitting room with my gun.

"All of you, into the living room. We're going to have a little chat."

Chapter Forty-Five

Penelope

"Before you accuse me of anything, you might want to look on the table," I said, smartly pointing toward the dining room.

I was already sitting in my usual wingback chair. Mother and daughter were on the couch, sitting closer than necessary. Aww, how sweet. I rolled my eyes.

"Why?" Lolly looked tired, dark circles under her eyes and sweat staining the pits of her long-sleeved shirt.

"Someone left us all another note earlier. I can give you the CliffsNotes version if you want. Basically, they said Bonnie was the killer," I grinned.

"You are such a moron," Bonnie said, shaking her head.

While Lolly went to the dining area to retrieve the note to read it for herself, I whispered to the others, "We could make a run for it." I pointed at the front door. "Or it's three against one, so we could ambush her if need be."

"I don't feel like getting shot in here or hacked to death out there. But thanks for the suggestion," Staci snapped.

I couldn't help it; I smiled at Staci. She was pretty witty sometimes on her channel, too. As much as I hated to admit it, I did sometimes watch the competition late at night when I was bored and feeling sorry for myself.

"I'm going to the bathroom," Bonnie said, getting to her feet.

"Wait…" I spoke.

"If I'm the killer, then I have nothing to worry about, right?" Bonnie said, giving me a furious look as she strolled into the dining area. I could hear an exchange between her and Lolly, Lolly threatening to shoot her if she tried to make a run for it after taking a piss.

Lolly entered the room, shaking the note in one hand and toting the gun in the other.

"I don't get it. Why would someone imply that Bonnie was the killer in this letter, and that I'm the killer in that stupid rhyme meant for me? It's almost like someone wants to confuse us…" Lolly pondered.

"That's because they do." Bonnie re-entered the room, carrying that heavy brass candlestick in her arms again. "The actual killer is trying to confuse everyone."

I started to say something, smart and witty, but mean nonetheless, but then Bonnie brought the candle down over my head. Darkness seeped in, my body sliding off the couch and sinking to the floor below.

Chapter Forty-Six

Bonnie

"What the hell did you do that for?" Staci screamed, jumping to her feet. Immediately, she was on the ground, leaning over Penelope's body.

"Drop that fucking candle," Lolly said, words slow and powerful, her eyes fully black and full of rage.

"No problem." I let the candlestick fall. It hit the hard floor with a thud and the hit echoed dully through the space.

"Is she breathing?" Lolly asked Staci, keeping her eyes trained on me.

"She is. And she's got a pulse. I think it just knocked her unconscious," Staci said. She checked and re-checked Penelope's pulse.

"My intention wasn't to kill her, just to incapacitate her for a bit," I said, gripping the back of the sofa with both of my hands to steady my shaking nerves. I'd never hurt anyone before now, but Penelope deserved it.

"Don't you all understand? It has to be her," I told them. When they gave me quizzical looks, I went on: "All three of us were out by the pool when someone attacked Rad. There was only one person left behind inside the house that could have snuck up on him. Her." I pointed down at Penelope.

"It could be anyone!" Staci shouted. "A psycho could be out there!" She pointed toward the front door.

I nodded. "That's possible, but there are other reasons I think it was her. That stupid letter we received earlier … each line was written for those in the room. Hers was the only line that wasn't insulting, remember? It just said something like, 'One of us likes to create stories', and then it dogged the rest of us. She must be the one who wrote it."

Neither woman looked convinced.

"She was also the only one in the house, besides me, when Cornelius vanished, and then wound up killed. And she was standing right outside the room with the false wall where we found his body when I came upstairs. I think the only reason she took me to him is because I caught her going into Staci's room."

Lolly shrugged. "Maybe…"

Staci stood up from the floor, brushing off her hands and knees. "You could be right, Bonnie. Or you could be wrong … but I have a different theory."

Chapter Forty-Seven

~TWO O'CLOCK~

Staci

"The way I see it is this: there was only one other person outside when Rad and I found Mary Beth's body. And only one person in our group who is still alive who wasn't mentioned at all in that note…" I turned my eyes toward Lolly. Her mouth was grim; she seemed to know where I was going with this.

"Rad found your drawings, Lolly. Before he died, he told me. They were dated from before the massacre. A creepy girl in the picture and there's an ax," I said.

"What drawings?" Bonnie asked, looking at me, and then at Lolly.

I looked at my mother, trying to make her understand. "Only one of us snuck in a gun. And only one of us is pointing it at everyone else. So, while I think your concerns about Penelope are valid, Bonnie, there is no one I trust less than her." I held an arm out and extended my finger, pointing it straight at Lolly.

Chapter Forty-Eight

Lolly

"Let me explain a few things," I said, taking a deep breath. I wandered over to the fireplace and placed the gun down on the mantle. I wasn't a gun person, never had been. But I'd spent so long in survival mode that I didn't know how to get out of it, even if I wanted to. I bought a gun right after Sadie was born, determined to keep her safer than my parents kept me.

"Tell us, Lolly. We're listening," Bonnie said, quietly. She motioned for Staci to come over and sit beside her, but Staci sat down on the floor beside Penelope's unconscious body instead, resting a hand on her shoulder. Her chest was still moving up and down, so that was a good thing. As crude as the woman was, I didn't want her to die. I didn't think that Bonnie wanted her to die either…

None of us were killers. Were we?

"I was troubled when I was young. This is no secret for those who knew me. My father drank heavily, and my mother was sick all the time. I was left alone to fend for myself most days. And I spent a lot of time in my own head, drawing. Thinking. Sometimes I came here alone. And sometimes I came with other kids from school. The kids who died here weren't really my close friends. In fact, they bullied me often. But it's not like you can speak ill of the dead, right? Now I'm getting off track…"

My temples were throbbing. I massaged them, but continued pacing. Talking.

"I drew lots of dark things. Nothing too dark, not really. But that's how I expressed myself. And you have to remember … this was the nineties. Kids my age were just getting exposed to the best horror movies Hollywood had to offer… Michael Myers. Jason Voorhees. Well, you get my point. So, yes there was an ax in one of my drawings. There were knives and witches and demons and all kinds of things, but those drawings weren't included…"

I took a breath and looked solemnly at Bonnie and Staci.

"But I do think it's strange that I left that particular notebook, with those particular drawings stashed here at my favorite place. The cops didn't find them after the murders—trust me, I was worried they would, and they'd think I was a psycho and arrest me. But they never did. I never saw the drawings again until two weeks ago, when they showed up at my front door in an envelope … that's why I came. I knew the killer, or someone who knew more than they were letting on, was responsible for bringing us here. I wanted to see what their motives were and figure out how they got those drawings from all those years ago. Make sense?"

Bonnie nodded her head, but Staci still looked skeptical.

"On the night of the murders in 1996, I hid in one of my favorite hiding spots. That's how I escaped the killer. Instead of helping my friends, I ran. There's a concrete hatch in the ground near the pool that opens into a small storage space for keeping supplies and pool floats... who knows what it was originally for, but that's what me and my friends used it for when we used to hang out here That's where I was earlier. I opened the hatch and hid down that storage space out there by the pool, right after I went to the guest house and found Mary Beth. Her blood was all over the floor... After a while though, sitting down in that dank space in the dark ... I decided that I had to come out. I'm sick of hiding. I've spent too much of my life hiding…"

"And the gun?" Staci pressed.

"I hid it in there, too."

"What? When?" Bonnie said, doubts crossing her face for the first time.

"Two weeks ago," I admitted.

"Excuse me?" This time from Staci.

"There's a tear in the fence about a mile down the fence line from here… It was there when I was a kid, and it was still there when I went back two weeks ago. I wasn't taking any chances. I knew that the likelihood of the killer being here was high. Or at least someone with ill intentions. So, I snuck inside a couple of weeks ago, right after signing that

NDA… I took a look around the property. No one was here. And then I stored my gun in the hiding spot, as well as some flashlights and first aid supplies. Just in case. When you've been through a lot of shit like I have, you plan ahead for trouble," I explained.

Staci's face softened.

"Our pasts do shape us. No doubt about that," Bonnie said.

"You could have run earlier, followed the fence line a mile and escaped through the fence," Staci said.

I nodded. "That's what I planned to do when the sun came up, or earlier if I got the chance, but then I decided that I needed to know the truth. I needed to see which one of you was the killer."

"Well, it's not me," Staci said.

"Not me either," said Bonnie.

I wanted to believe them; really, I did.

"Are we sure she's okay?" I asked, pointing at Penelope on the floor.

"I hope so. I still don't trust her. I've had a sick feeling about her in my gut since we arrived." Bonnie spoke softly.

I bent down and re-checked Penelope's pulse. It was thready, but it was definitely there. The rise and fall of her chest was also a good sign.

As carefully as possible, I lifted her head and inspected where Bonnie had hit her.

"I'm sorry. I just…" Bonnie pleaded from the couch.

I put up a hand to shush her. "There's a goose egg-sized knot on the back of her head. Let's find her something in the kitchen, maybe a bag of frozen peas, or anything really cold will work. We need to wake her up soon, in case she is concussed…"

In an unspoken pact, the three of us moved toward the kitchen together in tandem. By the time we made it and started searching through the dank, old freezer for something cold enough to use on Penelope's head, it was too late to go back for the gun. I'd placed it on the mantle while talking earlier, letting my guard down.

It'll be okay. Neither of these women can hurt me, I attempted to soothe myself.

Right on cue, I heard the shuffle of feet and I startled at the thump of a door being closed.

"I thought you locked it," I said, looking back and forth between Bonnie and Staci. Both were wide-eyed and scared, all three of us frozen in place as we waited to see who was here to kill us.

Chapter Forty-Nine

Bonnie

"Hello!" came a man's voice, a voice I didn't recognize. I shot a perplexed look at Staci and Lolly.

"Who the hell is that?" I hissed.

"Hello … oh no, oh…" We heard rapid shuffling and then sounds of what sounded like sobbing.

"Where's the gun?" Staci whispered, nudging Lolly.

"I left it in there, with him. Whoever he is," Lolly said, through clenched teeth.

"I'll go first," I offered. "I'll distract him, while you run over and get your gun back, okay?

Lolly nodded, and the three of us walked slowly back toward the front room.

Could it be someone coming to relieve us? Our actual host

this time? Please don't be a killer, I thought, dread circling my chest.

"Who are you?" I demanded, entering the room and nodding at Lolly to go for the gun.

A man I'd never seen before was sitting on the cold, hard floor, trying to shake Penelope awake.

He looked up at me, startled. I glanced over at Lolly just as she gripped the gun in her hands.

"Tell us who you are, or I'll shoot you. Don't move, or I'll shoot you. Do you understand me?" Lolly shouted, aiming the gun in his direction.

The man leaned back on his heels and held his hands in the air. "I'm Robert. Robert Jewel. I'm Penelope's husband."

"How do we know you aren't lying?" I asked.

"He's not." Staci moved to stand next to me. "I've seen Robert before, in videos and in the newspaper. He attends events with Penelope sometimes. But how did you know Penelope was injured?" Staci asked.

All eyes turned to Robert. He was tall and broad-shouldered, elderly, like Penelope. Perhaps a few years younger than her. His hair was thin and graying, but he looked essentially harmless. I wouldn't really know unless I got closer to him though… I needed to see if I could pick up on his vibe.

I shuffled a few inches forward, hoping Lolly would shoot him if he tried anything.

"I didn't know. She was okay when I talked to her … well, if you consider being trapped in the house with a murderer okay," he said, narrowing his eyes suspiciously at each of us.

"You talked to her?" I asked, scooting closer still. There was something off about him ... but I couldn't figure out what it was.

"She called me. She snuck a cell phone in with her, sewed it inside her bag. I could barely hear her when she called but she said that she found a dead body in the wall. And that there were others ... that all of you were in danger."

"Cornelius," I said, nodding. "I was with Penelope. We found him together. And she was telling the truth. Others are dead," I swallowed, fighting off images of Rad's mangled body out there in the tunnel.

"She's breathing but I don't know ... did one of you do this to her?" Robert leaned his face over Penelope's, pressing his lips to her and whispering soothing words to his wife.

I felt my walls coming down.

"I can't believe she had a phone this whole time," I said, glancing at the other women to get their thoughts.

"If that's the case, why didn't she call the cops?" Lolly hadn't lowered the gun, and she was staring at Robert strangely, still assessing him with those hard, black eyes of hers. When she was angry, she looked like a whole other person to me.

"Because I called them for her, while we were on the phone together. From our landline phone. The cops are already on their way. They should be here any minute. But

Penn and I don't live far from here, so I just jumped in the car and got here as fast as I could. Want to take that gun off me? I'm not worried about myself, but I don't want my wife getting shot when she's already clearly injured. What happened to her, by the way?"

I opened my mouth to tell the truth, but my daughter spoke up for me.

"After we found Rad—that's one of the other houseguests—we were all so scared and we took off running. Penelope slipped and hit the floor hard. We were just going to put these on her bump" Staci stepped forward and tossed a bag of frozen mixed vegetables on the floor next to Robert.

"Thank you," he said, gently lifting his wife's head with one hand and sliding the bag of vegetables under it with the other. "I think she'll be okay. I hope..." he said. His teary eyes and the wobble in his voice seemed genuine, but I still didn't trust this stranger.

I wasn't sure if I trusted anyone except Staci.

"How did you get in? The door was locked," Lolly said.

Robert pulled his hands away from his wife and shrugged at Lolly. "It wasn't. I turned the knob and came right in."

"Did one of you forget? I thought we locked it earlier," Lolly said, glancing at me. She nodded over to the door, motioning for me to check.

"Regardless, we need to lock it now. At least until the cops get here," I said. I walked over to the door, stepping around Penelope on the floor and Robert in his hunched position, and I checked the deadbolt. It was unsecured. Quickly, I locked it again then double-checked that I'd done it right.

When I turned back around, I noticed Robert's backside. There was a bulge under his t-shirt, something tucked in the back of his waistband. *Another gun to deal with?*

But before I could say anything, Robert started talking. I took a step closer, trying to get a better look at the bulge.

"It's always good to lock your doors," Robert was saying. He was looking at Lolly as he said it. "My father was a hunter and he raised me to be one too. Have you ever hunted before?"

Lolly was frozen where she stood, gun in hand, watching the man with a look of unease. She didn't answer his question.

I pointed at his back and tried to catch Lolly's eye, but she was watching him so intensely, laser-focused. Staci caught my eye though and I pointed again at the suspicious thing in his pants.

"We used to have our best chats up in the tree stand, my dad and I," Robert said, brushing the hair off Penelope's face. "It was in that very stand that I admitted to him I was being bullied. A mean pack of teenage boys. You know the type." He glanced up at Lolly again.

I noticed the gun shaking wildly in her hands. "Lolly…"

"My father said," Robert boomed loudly, drowning me out, "'son, this land is full of lions. And they like to move in packs. You can kill or maim them but it's no matter; there will always be more lions waiting to take their place.' He told me then … 'son, my best advice is that you figure out where their dens are. Once you know that, you must learn to avoid those dens.' Good advice, right?"

Robert finally took his eyes off Lolly and glanced back at me with a sheepish smile. "Sorry, I talk when I'm nervous," he said, but he didn't look nervous at all. Not to me. There was something else there, brimming under the surface … straight adrenaline coursing through his veins.

"I remember that speech," Lolly said, her words slow and deliberate. "I remember the first time you gave it to me, standing out there in those woods." She nodded toward the door.

"Oh, good. I was hoping you remembered, Lolly," Robert said, petting his wife again.

I glanced over at Staci, my fears at an all-time high. *Go, baby. Run.* I mouthed those words to my daughter, and she seemed to understand. She started slinking off toward the side hallway, ready to make an escape through the side tunnel that led outside.

"But that's the problem with lions," Lolly said, stepping forward with the gun. "Sometimes, even when you avoid their dens, they still turn up and walk straight into your house."

"What should you do then?" Robert said, his expression positively gleeful. I backed up, trying to get closer to the front door, planning my own escape…

"You take them out," Lolly said. She stepped forward again with the gun, and this time she pulled the trigger.

Chapter Fifty

~THE WITCHING HOUR~

Staci

Torn between running and staying, I stopped at the entrance to the hallway, waiting to see what would happen. I wasn't sure what was going on with Penelope's husband, exactly, but I knew it wasn't good. His entire demeanor had changed: concerned about Penelope those first few minutes, strange and eerie the next.

"Lolly, wait," I tried to choke out the words. But it was too late; I could see that she was going to shoot him, just by the flick of fury in her eyes.

But when she pulled the trigger nothing happened. *Click.*

Lolly looked down at the gun in her hand, confusion flooding her face; she stumbled back as Robert got to his feet, and then she cocked it and tried to fire again. *Click.*

Click. Click. Click.

The gun wasn't firing at all.

"All this time, you thought I didn't know about your hidey hole, but of course I did. I let you live because there always has to be one … a final girl, as they call them. I didn't expect you to bring a gun, which was a sweet surprise. But I found it before you even got here, and of course I unloaded the bullets," Robert said.

As he reached around behind his back, I finally saw what my mother had been trying to show me only moments earlier. Robert was carrying an ax.

He slipped it out and brought it around to show Lolly. "An old friend," he said, running his finger across the sharp edge of the blade.

My mother was moving, her hand slowly turning the lock, reaching for the door. I prepared myself to run in the other direction … the tunnel would take me outside, away from this psychotic man…

As though he could sense it, Robert spun on his heels. "And where do you think you're going, fraudster? You're next on my list."

I watched, in horror, as Robert ran at my mother, ax blade slicing through the open air. She cried out, holding up her hands in defense, but it was no match for the blade.

There was a sick, wet sound and a wounded cry, and then my mother slumped down to the floor. I stared at her face, cheek pressed to the cold floor, dead eyes aimed straight at me, where I was hiding in the shadowy hallway. Blood bubbled around her lips, a stream of blood leaking from her mouth and travelling across the floor like a red river of pain.

I cried out in horror, covering my mouth with my hands.

Lolly's wide, frantic eyes flashed over to mine. We locked eyes. "Go now, Staci! Run!" she screamed.

I turned on my heels and took off down the hallway, Lolly's screams following behind me in the dark.

I don't remember moving through the tunnel, but I must have fallen several times. Once, over Rad's dead body. I burst through the exit, into the cold night air, and ran straight for the trees. I ran and ran, never stopping, following the tree line as far as I could, branches slapping at my cheeks, cutting through my shirt and pants ... thorns catching in my hair and clothes.

Lolly had promised that there was a tear in the fence a mile ahead. I would run a thousand miles if I had to in order to reach it...

I wouldn't stop running until I got some help for my mother, my friend ... and until I found my own freedom on the other side of this fence, away from this hellscape castle.

Chapter Fifty-One

Lolly

"I'm sorry it couldn't be you this time," Robert said, using his shirt to wipe the blood from his face, and to wipe down his vicious ax.

"What are you talking about?" I said, desperately, fumbling to open the chamber of the gun to check it. *Fuck. He's right, no bullets. Asshole!*

"I'm talking about Staci. She's younger and faster. Has her whole life ahead of her ... unlike you and her." He nodded over at Bonnie, what was left of her on the floor.

I closed my eyes, refusing to look. I stared past her, focusing my eyes elsewhere ... not wanting to see the severed flesh, the blood gushing in streams across the castle floor.

"Fuck you," I said, looking around desperately for a

weapon within reach. I could hit him with the butt of the gun to defend myself, but it wasn't much against an ax.

That might be my only choice though, I thought, mind swirling with desperation. *I'll fight until I win, or I'll die trying.*

"I had to let Staci go this time. There can only be one final girl. And you already had your chance at that … there's no second-chance final girls, Lolly."

"Please." I put my hands up as Robert moved closer with the ax, swinging it by his side. "I remember you from back then, I do. That speech in the woods … I thought you were helpful. I thought you were…"

"A good guy?" Robert said with a smug smile. "The world isn't divided by good and evil, Lolly. It's a lot murkier than that."

"Pretty sure ax murderers, especially ones who kill children, are bad guys by anyone's standards," I snapped.

He could try to kill me … hell, maybe he'd do it, too. But I wouldn't go down without a fight. All those years ago, I'd hidden in the alcove by the pool. But I wasn't hiding anymore. If Sadie grew up without a mother, at least she would know that I fought for my fucking life, trying to stay in this world with her. I'd gouge his eyes out on my way out, dig into his skin and blood with my nails, making sure there was plenty of DNA to catch him in this modern age…

"But why? I saw you in the woods a few times. You were always nice to me. Why kill my friends? And why kill these people now? What's the point? What did they do to deserve it?" My back connected with the sharp corner of the fireplace. There was nowhere else to go, and he was coming closer...

"We both know those kids weren't your friends. They bullied you; I saw them. And I watched you when you were alone, too. You were much happier here, without them. And that story I told about the lions, I meant it. You kept returning to their den, letting them tease you ... letting those boys take advantage of you, too."

"You're right. They were assholes. But they were kids. They didn't deserve to die. And I didn't ask for your help."

I'd told the police about him all those years ago, mentioning the anonymous hunter in the woods and the kid hanging around sometimes too, that kid was Bobby Reeks. But I never thought the hunter—this man—was the one who killed my friends. He was completely unrelated to Bobby, and I'd just assumed he was a normal townie scoping out the woods for deer. I had no idea, back then, that he was married to Penelope Jewel.

That night, the killer's face was covered in a mask, and I ran and hid so quickly ... never seeing my pursuer, not really. But now, I was learning that he never meant to pursue me at all. I didn't get lucky with my escape; he chose to let me live.

"So, bringing us here tonight ... you did all this for me again? But why, Robert?"

Robert laughed so hard he leaned forward and back on the balls of his feet, spittle flying.

"What the hell is so funny?" I demanded.

"It was never about you, Lolly. Not really. You aren't

that damn special, hate to break it to you," Robert guffawed. "I did you a favor when I killed those kids, and I enjoyed watching you. I even enjoyed doing the killings and all of the press and the chaos that ensued in our town afterwards. But I did it for Penelope."

"Penelope? I don't understand," I said.

"My dear wife is sharp as a tack. She gets people, she truly does. But she's always had a blind spot for me. She thinks of me as her dutiful servant, her sweet and giving husband. The bringer of coffee and tea and croissants. For many years, I went everywhere with her, traveling for book tours and events. But then, her career started to spiral, and I stayed home more, trying to find other ways to keep her happy. The first time I came out to these woods, I was looking for exotic flowers and plants. I built her a garden and she loved it..."

"How sweet," I said, dully.

"But she was still unhappy. I thought if I could give her something ... something new to work on, something closer to home ... that she would finally be content. With the first massacre, I was so sure she'd get to write the true crime story ... but she was passed over for it.

"She researched you; did you know that? And the others too. She was obsessed by this case but she never knew that the real killer was beside her all along."

"But why now? Why do this again if you got away with it the first time?" I asked.

"Don't you see? This whole night was my present to her. My final gift."

"What a great gift," I muttered, clenching my hands into fists. I wanted to beat him bloody, tear the evil, black heart from his chest. If I had my own ax, I'd swing it straight toward his face then lodge it deep in thick, dumb skull.

"I was certain she would get to write the story about my first killings, especially since the Beechwood Massacre was local for her. But they screwed her over and it devastated her. This time ... they won't dare tell her no," Robert chuckled.

"Let me guess. They can't say no because this time she'll be able to write the story about her own husband, a murderer living under her own roof all these years ... a murderer who planned this sick and twisted game in her honor," I said, spitting out the words in disgust.

"That's where you're wrong, Lolly. This won't come back to me. I got away with it once, and I'll get away with it again. I cleaned up behind you last time, did you know that? I painted over your angry words on the wall. Hid your crazy drawings from the cops. I was going to use a gun to kill your friends ... but then I saw that drawing you made, the one with the ax and ... well, you made me feel inspired, Lolly. But I no longer need inspiration from you...

"You're insane! Staci's on her way out of here right now. It's only a matter of time before she reaches the cops."

Robert laughed. "You of all people should know how long that hike takes. After all, you ran all those miles yourself once upon a time, during your heyday as the final girl, my dear. No second chances this time."

"Still. They're coming, whether you like it or not. You

can kill me, but you'll still get caught. There are no second chances with ax murderers either, asshole."

"Wrong again, Lolly. By the time the police get here, I'll have all my I's dotted and my T's crossed. The ax used to kill Cornelius and that hostess I hired is in Staci's room. Her DNA is all over the place out there from when she discovered the body. And I've already typed a note, hidden in her bag for them to find. A manifesto, of sorts. A troubled young girl with mental health issues tries to recreate a heinous crime to gain more fame for herself ... it wouldn't be the first time she made up lies to gain viewers and attention. It's brilliant, really,"

"It's sick and no one will believe you," I said. He was so close now, too close. I prepared myself for the fight of my life...

As he lunged for me, I threw a punch, connecting with his nose. He stumbled backwards but I did too; and looking down, I saw the gash on my shoulder, deep red blood oozing out from it. I gripped my arm and moved forward, holding my arms up, hands gripped into fists.

"I expected you to be tougher," Robert laughed, wiping blood from his nose. "But that punch was weak."

"You're weak. A stupid, weak, little man. You might have overestimated me, but I think you underestimated her." I pointed behind him.

"Who?" Robert said, turning to look at his wife.

Chapter Fifty-Two

Penelope

When I opened my eyes, head throbbing with dull pain, I looked over and saw the unthinkable. My husband, Robert, swinging a hatchet like a stone-cold maniac, hacking up Bonnie Black to bits. Sure, I wanted revenge for what she did to me—my head felt like it was full of rocks—but this was taking it to the extreme, even by my standards.

After he murdered Bonnie, my dear sick husband was too busy running his mouth, patting himself on the back ... to notice I was moving on the floor. Pulling myself to my feet.

"Darling! You're awake!" Robert exclaimed, as soon as he turned and saw me. The look of delight on his face almost stopped me in his tracks. Say what you will about Robert, but his love for me has always been real.

"Yes, I'm awake. But you're about to go to sleep." I swung the pipe wrench, smacking him with a hard thwack across the face. Robert fell sideways, his oversized body hitting the floor with a painful thump. I let go of the wrench. It hit the floor with a clank and right away, Lolly dove down and grabbed it.

"But … I did it for you, darling. This is my love letter to you. Don't you understand?" Robert rasped, knobby fingers and arms reaching out for me from the floor. There was a bloody fissure in the center of his forehead, expanding to the top of his skull. Blood and fluid leaked from the wound I had caused, the moment becoming almost surreal.

I covered my mouth with my hands, barely breathing. *Oh, Robert.* I knew he was sick, and I think that, deep down, he knew that I knew, too. But I never expected him to go this far. The Beechwood Massacre…

I uncovered my mouth. "You did it for yourself, Robert. It was always about you, and satiating your own sick needs … this time, you went too far."

"No, daffodil," he choked out the words. "That's not true…"

I nodded to Lolly, then turned my back so I wouldn't see.

But I could hear her … Lolly Andrews slamming the wrench, again and again, over Robert's head until he was dead.

Chapter Fifty-Three

~SIX MONTHS LATER~

Staci

I t came as a surprise to no one that there was very little fanfare when we left the castle. There were no big, fancy checks with photographers standing by. No bursts of confetti when I exited the Beechwood property, panting like a wild dog in heat.

No popping of corks. No champagne. No prizes announced.

The whole money bit was a lie, just like the rest of it, all constructed by the sick mind of Robert Jewel, Rock Hill's very own ax murderer.

However … two weeks after I'd nearly died, I did get another NDA in the mail. Along with a special offer. A nice-sized check from the estate of Robert and Penelope Jewel, as long as I agreed not to sue the estate or draft a story about my time spent in the castle.

The first thing I did after I cashed it was give some money to my brother and sister-in-law. Then I thanked them for everything they'd done for me, packed all my meager shit in a U-Haul, and moved 700 miles away from Rock Hill.

I didn't tell Jan goodbye in person, but I did send her a text. I told her I was sorry for what I'd done, and I hoped that someday, maybe, we could be friends again. I wished her all the best with her makeup business. She had every reason to be upset with me, but at least she wasn't at the castle—and a possible victim—of Robert Jewel.

The house I bought isn't fancy—just a simple bungalow in a coastal town, not too far from New Orleans. According to my mother's sister—my only biological aunt—I have a few cousins and a grandmother here, on my father's side. One day I plan to meet them, but not until I'm ready for that.

As it turned out, each of the houseguests, including our hostess Mary Beth Penner, were offered the same amount of money that I was from the Jewel estate. Since my mother was deceased, I was sent her portion, too.

Now I have more money than I'll ever know what to do with. Despite that, I still live like I'm poor—only buying what I need, week to week. Day to day. It's a habit that I don't know if I'll ever break.

My mother was cremated. I keep her ashes in a shiny, blue urn. One day I might take them to the boardwalk in Atlantic City or the marshlands of New Orleans and let them go. According to my aunt, she loved those cities, and she loved Cajun culture. But I also know she loved me.

Part of me thinks that she would prefer to stay right here for now, sitting on a bookshelf in my tiny new house, keeping me and the dog and the cats company while we work on these cold cases. It's strange, but I feel her energy here. Like she's in the room with me, whispering in my ear sometimes. I know that hearing voices isn't normal, but I've never been normal anyway.

Even though I can't write my story, per my NDA, I did use my funds to buy new equipment and to hire a couple of part-time staffers to help build my channel. It's growing daily and getting more attention than ever, thanks to my well-televised, near-death experience at the castle.

Now that I don't have to worry about my daily survival thanks to the blood money, I can focus on my true passion— finding the girls who go missing. The ones left behind and forgotten. Because I know what that feels like … to feel lost in a world where no one's searching, and no one seems to give a damn about where you are. But, sometimes, there's that one person … out there on the fringes, always looking out. Trying to track you down.

I don't know much about how the others are doing, but I did hear through my gossipy aunt back in Rock Hill that Cornelius Jones' wife and young children received money on his behalf. They, too, moved away from the town. Living somewhere on a beach, my auntie told me. And Rad—there was also news about him. Apparently, the ex-cop had no family, but he did have a living will, according to his long-time lawyer and friend. What little assets and money he had before his death, according to his will, were meant for Richard and Kelly Reeks, the parents of young Bobby Reeks, the boy whose death he was responsible for. So, it was only right that the money from the Jewel settlement should go to them, too. I didn't know the Reeks's personally, but I felt certain that no amount of money would make up for the loss of their son. But I was glad that the money went to a family that deserved it; a family that had gone through hell, just like the rest of us caught up in the storm of Robert Jewel's evil deeds.

I don't know what my future holds; I truly don't. There's a part of me that wants to climb under the covers and enable my expensive security cameras, and never leave the house again. That way I don't have to worry about all those lions out there … roaming around on this earth, waiting to make others their prey. But I'm fighting back against that impulse—because no amount of avoidance can truly keep me safe. I can't spend my whole life living in fear, worrying about what might happen next. Because, like Lolly said, sometimes the lion shows up and comes right in your house, even when you're hiding from them and trying to play it safe…

These days, I take my mental health meds as prescribed, and I focus on pursuing my passions. I try to make a small difference in the world. I know that's what my mother would have wanted…

Chapter Fifty-Four

Lolly

When I first learned about the offer from the Jewel estate, I planned to refuse it. But there were just too many zeros listed on that check to say no.

Sadie's future is more important than my ego.

So, I quit my job at Home Depot, hired extra care for Dad, and made some much-needed repairs to the house. That's what I did with the money, initially.

Last week, Sadie's school let out for summer break, and she turned fourteen on the same day. Instead of wrapping up gifts, I bought her something else—a big RV camper. *"Let's spend the summer traveling. You and me and Grandad. You point to a spot on the map, anywhere you want to go that we can reach by land, and that's where I'll take you. Let's go see everything, baby. Let's get away from this town,"* I told her.

Sadie was so excited and the first place she wants to go

is a place called Myrtle Beach. I've never been to the ocean, but I feel like I have. I've imagined it in my dreams.

I can't wait to get there … can't wait to taste the salty air. To feel the grit of sand between my toes. To feel the frothy burn of saltwater sweeping in and out, coating my ankles and shins.

Next, Sadie mentioned a city—maybe New York or Pittsburgh. I've never been to those places either. I imagine it will be amazing to look up, up, up at the tall buildings, like spires that touch that sky … and feel so small in the world. I just want to feel small again. Mostly, I want us all to be safe. I want men like Robert Jewel to not exist anymore.

My father isn't doing well. Every day his health deteriorates, but I'm taking him with us too. At least, for however long his health will allow it.

I know he wasn't the best father, and every part of me wants to just treat him as badly as he treated me when I was vulnerable and weak … but I'm not him, I'm me. And my daughter is watching. I won't let his past behavior impact my future—I'll take care of him, the way he should have cared for me when I needed a family to lean on. I will break the cycle and show my daughter that real families rush in; we help each other when we are needed.

Chapter Fifty-Five

Penelope

"Cheers." I lifted my champagne flute and clinked it against the others, smiling at my friends around the table.

Yes, friends. I guess I can call them that. At least this is better than the last dinner party I went to in that ninth circle of hell at the Beechwood estate.

Once again, I'm surrounded by friends and admirers. It's not that people like me again—I'm not that naïve—and I'm pretty sure they never did. It's because they are drawn to my success, like maggots are drawn to rotten flesh.

They can't get enough of me now that I have a big book deal and a mind-blowing new story, coming out to stores near you this November.

In six months, my new book will enter the world

—*Living with a Monster: The Untold Story of Robert Jewel.* Written by his wife, of course.

After I nearly died in that castle, and the news of my husband's evil acts exploded on every news outlet, my agent and editors came rushing to my side to ask what I planned on doing next.

I played hardball, asking for lots of money. Not because I need it, but because I'm me.

I want them to respect me again.

I want this, I thought, looking around the fancy table, with its linen cloth covering and expensive dishes loaded with seafoam salad and steak tartar, my favorites.

Since Robert's death and the signing of the deal, I've been very hush hush about the upcoming story. I don't want to give any spoilers and I've refused to share any details with even those close to me, agents or editors. If they want to hear it all, then they'll have to buy the book, too, when it gets here in November.

But people on the street stop me everywhere. They ask me the same question, again and again: *how did you not know? With your background, didn't you suspect…?*

Absolutely not, I tell them. Then I force myself to hang my head and move on.

But it's a lie, all of it.

Did I know that my husband of forty years was an ax murderer? No, not exactly. But Lolly was right about one thing—he did underestimate me.

Of course I saw his darkness.

Of course I knew he was different than others … just like me.

I watched him turn on his charm with everyone else, getting into character. But he never did that with me—his charm with me was real. For all Robert's many faults, not loving me wasn't one of them.

That man adored me, and I do miss him.

I plan to write about that—very carefully—in the upcoming book. I want to make myself look human after all; showing a little vulnerability might help my sales.

Mostly, the story will involve unearthing the true Robert Jewel. I'm currently in the process of doing research, learning things about who he was before we met, things I didn't know about his childhood or early life before we came to be partners. I'm also retracing all of our steps taken together over the last forty years.

I didn't suspect that he was the Beechwood killer. Not right away, at least.

But there were times when I wondered … women gone missing when we travelled to Vancouver. A strange murder in Pensacola, fewer than six miles from where I was doing a conference back in 2006. My point is … I knew he was capable of it. But I never questioned him. He gave me my space and I gave him … my trust—it's one of the most important elements of a marriage.

But when I got to the castle that night and I looked around the table at all those faces, and I added up the guestlist … I knew that something was going on. Because

I'd researched each and every single one of them. Each, at one point, was the subject of a failed pitch line, or rejected story idea. I knew that whoever brought us there had brought those guests specifically for me. And I only admitted my failures to one person in this world and that was my darling Robert.

That night at the castle, when Rad mentioned the LLC he'd discovered in Massachusetts, it solidified Robert's guilt for me. Because I remembered that dinky storefront. It had a crooked sign on the front of it, and it was part of one of those band-aid-clusterfuck, strip mall things. "Why the hell did you buy this?" I asked him.

It's not that we couldn't afford it, but I didn't see why he wanted the space. We loved Massachusetts, staying at the Ocean Cliff Hotel and visiting The Berkshires, but our home was in Indiana. And what did we need a shitty little store like that for?

Robert claimed it was for "someday", a place to sell his plants and flowers. That stupid man deemed himself an artist when it came to gardening. I couldn't stop laughing when he showed it to me, honestly. It was the first time he'd truly looked angry with me, but he got over it quickly. He always did.

Over the years, I'd brought it up—that dinky little place in Massachusetts. I offered to let him open a shop there, on days when I was feeling nice. But he always denied having an interest in it. "It was a silly idea. Never mind," he would say. But he never sold the property. It stayed vacant all those years, and the utilities were paid for regularly from our accounts.

"Penelope, hi!" Two producers, Shawn and Gary, walked hand in hand toward the table. We were supposed to have a meeting—the book wasn't finished yet, but there was already talk of a movie, or documentary series.

"Well, hello. Nice of you all to finally join us," I said, glancing harshly at my diamond watch. If they wanted to woo me, then they should at least show up on time.

"Sorry. We were printing out some lists. Getting the numbers for you. Ready to talk business?" Gary said, sliding into the seat next to mine.

"Always," I said, giving him a shrewd smile over the top of my glass.

This was what I wanted, and Robert would have wanted this too … but I had to admit, that I missed him.

"I still can't believe you were married to that murderer." Shawn leaned in from my other side. His breath stunk of booze and cigarettes.

"Gary! Have some couth, man," his partner warned.

I set my drink down and waved him off. "No worries, my dear. I like people who say what's on their mind, as long as they have a good one." I smiled at drunken Shawn, then knocked gently on his stupid head with my knuckles.

"He was a monster indeed. A heartless, ruthless killer. But, in his defense, he was married to me. The only thing worse than being married to a murderer is being married to a writer."

I watched the faces around the table, the grimaces and

uncomfortable shifting in their chairs ... but then one of them started laughing and the next thing I knew, the entire table was rolling with laughter at my joke.

Yes, this is the life ... no doubt about it. Robert would be proud.

Acknowledgments

I am forever grateful to my editor, Jennie Rothwell, for supporting my writing. Thank you for making me a better writer and for believing in me. I'm also grateful to my copyeditor, Dushi Horti, for all the small (and big) mistakes you catch! Thank you to all of the staff at One More Chapter and HarperCollins for working tirelessly behind the scenes and in front of the scenes to get my books in the hands of readers all over the world.

Thank you to my brilliant literary agent, Katie Shea Boutillier, and the Donald Maass Literary Agency, for supporting me every step of the way and being my biggest cheerleaders!

Most importantly, thank you to YOU, dear reader, for taking a chance on my books! Please leave me a review and let me know what you think.

Read on for an extract from Carissa Ann Lynch's novel *The Summer She Disappeared*.

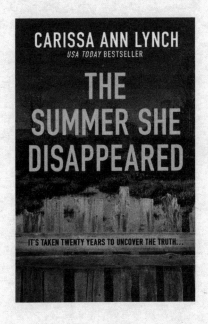

The Summer She Disappeared: Chapter 1

Want to see a dead body?

CURRENT DAY

There is a body in the bedroom closet.

Those were the words of the construction worker, the only female on the team.

Cindy. The woman's name is Cindy, I chastised myself.

I'd always been good with faces, terrible with names. And still, I didn't know most of the locals in Hillendale, much less the burly construction and home improvement crew I'd hired to work on my parents' lake house. *My house. It's my house now,* I reminded myself.

Cindy's words spun like a cyclone. Words buzzing in my brain, growing louder...

There is a body in the bedroom closet.

That can't be what she said. I must have simply misheard...

I followed the wooden planks of the foot bridge, eyes forward and hands firm on the gnarly, old handrails. By the time I reached the other side of the lake, feet anchored in the rich black soil of the forest, Cindy's garbled words had been reduced to nonsensical syllables in my brain.

I must have heard wrong. The connection was poor...

Halloween was still weeks away, too early for pranks. And Cindy didn't strike me as the trickster type. I'd only met her on two occasions, crossing paths on my first morning at the site and again last week when I did a surprise drop-by to check on the workers' progress. Cindy had stood out to me; of course she had, being the only woman in the group.

She seemed like a quiet woman, barely twenty, her eyes cast low, focused on her work as she poured a smooth, flat layer of concrete for the new patio. She was pretty, muscular but not too much so ... not like what you'd expect.

I shouldn't expect anything. It's not that weird, seeing an attractive young woman in that role, is it?

But tonight, Cindy had sounded different, her voice crackling on the other end of the line, her voice *frantic*, cutting hard as stone, raising to a feverish pitch as she relayed what she'd found at the small lake house my parents left me.

When the call came in, I was sitting in front of the television with the volume on low. That was the way I spent most nights since moving to the town of Hillendale after inheriting the lake house and leaving my husband Jason behind. A weathered paperback strewn across my lap; remnants of a TV dinner balanced lazily on the arm of the sofa; Jimmy Fallon's voice so low I had to strain my ears to catch the punchlines ... that's when the call came in.

"You have to come! Come right now," Cindy barked down the line.

That's when her voice turned to static, and that's when I knew—service at the lake house at 1 Daisy Lane was the worst—so terrible, that the crew claimed it was a "dead zone", and they often traveled to neighboring properties to make their calls, or to check their social media feeds.

"There's a body in the bedroom closet," she said, her voice fading in and out. And before I could ask her to repeat herself, she was gone.

The path curled through a tunnel of trees, cedar and pine. Then it split. *Left or right, west or east? Pick your poison my dear,* Kathi Jo's words came back to me, fluttering like moth wings, beating on my inner ear.

It was a moonless night, the kind that swallows up everything. The kind that makes you afraid of the dark.

West. West is best, of course, the memory of Kathi Jo followed me up the hilltop. I didn't need a light to find my way to the lake house. *My house. It's my house now.*

I could have walked the wooded trail with my eyes closed, even now, all these years later.

The wind howled, the night air freezing. The sort of cold that pierces bone and turns skin to goose flesh. I was underdressed, in a Grateful Dead t-shirt and ripped blue jeans, but I'd had the sense, at least, to put on thick socks and my hiking boots before leaving my apartment.

I followed the east trail past the creek, around a thick black boulder that looked like bigfoot hunched in the dark. I brushed the boulder's cold, slick surface with my fingers as I passed. *For luck. Always touch for luck…*

Over the hill, the lake house came into view.

Even now, thirty-something years later, the place still felt like home to me in so many ways…

There was nothing special about the lake house. In fact, some might call it downright ugly. A simple salt box at the edge of the forest, its sloped roof made of timber. Inside, the decorum from another era—or perhaps another life, altogether. A stag's head over the fireplace; a beaver and a large-mouthed bass on the wall. The furniture, all eighties styled … forever stuck in a forgotten era, when life was easier. Better.

It was a drafty old house, water stains on the ceilings. A cobweb for every corner. The sort of place reserved for slasher flicks and murder mysteries.

It used to give me chills, coming here as a child … but, slowly, the whole place grew on me—not the place, but the memories. Mama in her reading chair, skin soft and tissue-thin. Dad on the back deck, watching the lake through a gap in the forest.

See anything new, Daddy?

Nope. It's always the same. Peaceful. Unchanging. And that's why I love it here. The years go by, but the lake stands still. Nothing in Hillendale ever changes, Daddy would say.

A sliver of moonlight revealed itself, casting the lake house in spooky shadows, like something from a haunted house. The shadows around the forest grew longer, stretching endlessly in the dark.

Oh, but it did change, Dad. And it happened when I least expected it. Nothing stays the same, Dad, not even here ... especially *not here ... surely, deep down, you knew that, too.*

For the first time since returning to Lake Hillendale, I felt a flash of fear in my chest.

This place isn't safe. Too many dreadful things happened here, things I'll never forget.

As Cindy emerged from the front of the house, it occurred to me, for the first time, that she had no business being here. Not at this time of night.

Why was she working this late, at half-past midnight?

The crew often showed up early on weekdays, retiring by four or five. Her presence here was uncanny, and she appeared to be all alone as she approached me in the dark.

Silent and weightless, this gazelle-like creature with forearms like boulders, sauntered toward me. She looked bigger, stronger, than I had initially realized. Perhaps meeting her alone was a mistake, something I never would have done had it been one of her male counterparts asking me to come.

I should have called the police after receiving her call. That would have been the smart thing to do...

"There you are. Thank God you came." Cindy stepped into the moonlight; cigarette clinched between her teeth. She looked decades older than I remembered.

"I-I'm sorry," I told her. "The connection was bad. I couldn't hear your words, what you were saying…"

Cindy tossed the cigarette in the brush, opened her mouth, and repeated those dreadful words again. The ones I didn't want to hear; the ones she had shouted earlier into the phone.

"There is a body in the bedroom closet. I'm sorry if I was freaked out on the phone, ma'am, but I didn't know what else to do. It looks like it's been there a while. I got … I got scared."

But she didn't look scared at all.

I walked toward the front door of the lake house, my brain pinwheeling. This made no sense at all.

The only body that comes to mind…

Cindy was talking, directing me where to go. But it was another voice I heard, playful in my mind.

I could almost hear her—the ghost of Kathi Jo—her singsong voice floating on the wind.

Her lips tickling my earlobe: *Want to see a dead body?*

SUMMER OF '98

The first time I went to Lake Hillendale, I was only a few months old. I don't remember it, obviously, but those later years of my youth are seared into my brain. Riding my trike, pumping little legs around the cul-de-sac in front of my grandmother's house. Kathi Jo and the others … those late, sticky nights in Hillendale…

The lake house belonged to my father's mother and then it belonged to my parents.

Mom and Dad rented a pontoon boat one summer, strapping me in so tight that half my face disappeared in the life jacket, gasping for air. *Always gasping for air at that age.*

My early memories of the lake house were hazy, and mostly good. But that all changed the summer I turned thirteen. The summer of Kathi Jo Redfield.

The funny thing about those years … the way Mom and Dad talked about our yearly vacations made me feel like a spoiled little princess. The lake house, the boat, the way the water of Lake Hillendale glistened and shone like glass … the way they told it, it was something out of a fairytale.

It wasn't a fancy vacation destination. Just a drafty old house that belonged to my grandmother, two hours from our double-wide trailer in Branton. But since my parents owned it outright, it was the perfect family destination each summer.

For a while, I felt like royalty at the lake house. Like the luckiest girl in the world…

While my friends went to Europe and the Caribbean, or to Florida or South Carolina, every year, we drove a hundred miles west to Lake Hillendale.

Every year, it was just Dad, Mom, and me. We stayed at the house; it was our yearly adventure. Some years Dad rented a boat for a few days, so we could go out and swim and fish in the brackish-green waters of Lake Hillendale. Some years we couldn't afford it.

Most nights, we would gather round the fire pit, roasting hot dogs, and sticky marshmallows. Watching the logs turn from ash to dust. I wrote stories in my notebook and sometimes, when I could get one or both of my parents to listen, I shared them. Always frightening, always dark—always a bit of truth laced in the margins, between the lines of my stories…

You're a real mood killer, Willow, my mother said once, when she drank too much beer and brandy. That was the last time I shared one of my stories with her.

I would walk through the woods, during the day, mostly. Stumbling down the rocky hillside, following the path by memory. *Down, down, down* until I reached the water.

At the edge of the muddy shoreline, there was an old stone staircase that led down into the water. Only the first couple steps were visible; the rest underwater, mossy and dark, like the entrance to a crumbly, cursed pool, or an ancient underwater cavern.

I would travel down the steps slowly, trying to anchor my feet to the stone for as long as I could, trying to see how deep I could take them underwater, but I always floated up before reaching the bottom.

The inside of the house was a creamy egg-shell blue. I hated the dead animals on the walls at first: the stag and the beaver; the angry eagle. Their glass eyes black and warning, watching me all the time. The animals came with the house, apparently. Just something we had to live with during our summers. Because Dad refused to let Mom take them down after Grandma passed away.

I hated those animals. But then I liked to remind myself of fairytales. Fairytales are rarely pretty, not when you strip them down to their bones. Snow White, or *Sneewittchen* as she was called in the original story, the German one, was saved by a rugged huntsman. I liked to imagine the house were his, these animals his trophies. And in this freezing cold house on the edge of the forest covered in vines, with the dead creatures on the wall and the green-black waters and the mossy rooftop with its green cloud cover ... that is where we fall in love in my story. That is where the hunter restrains himself, refusing to cut out my beating heart as a prize for the evil queen. *Take that, Wicked Queen!*

Grandma had kept the place sparsely furnished, a threadbare couch in one corner, a Lazy Boy chair in the other. There was a dining area, small kitchenette, and the main bedroom reserved for my parents.

Then, upstairs, upstairs was my world. A loft, the ceiling so low and slanted that I'd hit my head if I stood up straight. And the big mattress on the floor with the burly old blankets, my own little summer nest.

I liked it up there, stretched out on my back, thighs sticky with sweat because the AC didn't reach that high, watching the lake water swirl back and forth, back and forth, from my balcony view of the water. Glittery and magical, the image like a silent lullaby.

When the house was quiet, and I was sure my parents

were sleeping, I'd go out on the balcony and lie flat on my back, trying to avoid splinters while I counted the stars. Thinking about boys. Touching myself; even, once, going as far as to get fully undressed, the moonlight my only spectator.

Luckily, I was fully clothed on the first night I saw Kathi Jo Redfield. I wish I could say the same for her.

Flat on my back, I turned my head to the side, looking out over the water. The sideways view was disorienting from the balcony, my world tipped on its side like a tilt-o-whirl.

Something was stirring out there ... a change in the wind or a rustle in the trees, so succinct that I couldn't put my finger on it.

But that's when I saw it.

Something. No ... *someone.*

Someone was out there, head bobbing in the water. For a moment, I let the fantasies take hold. A mermaid. No, a *merman.* A Loch Ness Monster that transforms into a sexy young siren...

But this was no mythical beast. Dark tendrils of hair swirled around her head. And she was coming closer, and closer still ... lifting herself from the water, body glittering in the cool night air, as she slowly ascended the stone staircase, one step at a time, and entered the muddy banks of the deep dark lake.

Cattails parted as she moved up the hillside, gliding over the rocky terrain and zigzagging through the brush. Then, suddenly, she was standing in my own backyard, water dripping in rivulets down her naked body.

All this time, watching her emerge like a ghostly maiden, I hadn't moved a muscle. I was still sprawled on my backside, cheek pressed flat to the wooden slats of the decking, barely breathing.

The girl stopped in the center of the yard, hands resting on the grooves of her curvy hip bones. She was neither woman nor girl, but like me, stuck in that awful in-between. But she was nothing like the girls from Parker Valley Middle School. Even in the dark, I could tell.

I could see the glint of her piercings. Five holes in each ear, a hoop spread over both nostrils, like an angry bull. Eyes large, blue maybe ... and she had choppy black hair, wet and plastered to her skull.

There was something black on her left thigh, too, a large tattoo ... something angry and tentacled. She reminded me of a big wet butterfly, a specimen under glass.

The girl cleared her throat, stood her ground. It was then that my chest seized with terror. Surely, she couldn't see me all the way up here in the dark...

"Take a picture. It'll last longer," she crooned, her voice soft but raspy.

My lips parted to say something, perhaps to apologize ... but I found that my mouth was full of bees.

I couldn't see her smile in the dark, but I could hear it when she said, "Yoo-hoo, I see you up there."

My eyes squeezed shut, my cheeks blazed with embarrassment. Although, it made no sense; it was she who was trespassing, she who was naked … why did I feel like a creepy voyeur?

"Fine. Just lie there then," she sighed, bored with me now.

I heard movement in the grass, twigs snapping. I kept my eyes closed, held my breath, forced myself to count to 100. And when I opened them, she was gone. As though she'd never been there to begin with, just a butterfly of the lake, another piece of my homespun fairytale.

I woke to the smells of my mother's cooking. Eggs, over easy. Bacon, burned. And, maybe, jam on toast today. I sat up on my mattress, stretching, trying to reach the top of the loft with the tips of my fingers from where I sat on the bed. And that's when I remembered: the girl.

I took my time getting dressed. Everything at this age felt like effort, too much. I shimmied into a pair of jean shorts. Tugged a Rolling Stones t-shirt over my head.

By the time I plodded downstairs and slunk through the living room to the kitchen, hoping for coffee, I'd forgotten the girl again. But then, there she was. Standing in the middle of my parents' summer kitchen. Not a nighttime phantom, not an apparition. She was a real-life girl.

"There she is!" My mother was wearing her fake smile, the one she reserved for guests.

"Willow, this is Kathi Jo and her mom, Isabella! This is my daughter, Willow."

Kathi Jo looked different in the light of day, no longer the midnight harpy. Her choppy black waves were tucked back in a tight ponytail at the base of her neck. Her face looked softer, a splattering of freckles on her nose and cheeks. Her mother, on the other hand, looked nothing like her: tall where Kathi Jo was short, and hair white blonde, straight as a pin.

"Hi there," I said, quietly. I could feel the harpy staring, studying me. But I refused to meet her eye. *Again, why do I feel like I did something wrong? She's the weirdo, standing buck naked in my backyard,* I questioned myself.

There was a long pause, awkward and strained. My mother jumped to fill that space.

"We are thrilled to finally have some neighbors! I mean, we don't live here year-round, but we summer here every … well, summer," my mother said. My mother was an awkward woman, despite how hard she tried not to be.

Standing next to Kathi Jo's mother, my mother looked like a round little troll. My mother, with her glasses and tiny white teeth. She fluttered around the kitchen with nervous anxiety, talking to our guests.

"Ah. So, this is just your summer home?" the woman asked, giving my mother a sly smile then looking at me. I rolled my eyes, looking around for my father to save me.

I waited for my mother to tell them that this was actually our grandmother's house and we lived in the Branton trailer park in Boone County. But she decidedly failed to mention that part.

"Ummm … sort of," my mother said.

I cut in, "Did you just move here?" I looked at the woman, eyes sliding over to look at the girl. *Kathi Jo. Sounds like a redneck name to me,* I thought.

"Yeah, we bought the house next door." Kathi Jo jabbed a thumb, indicating the big, gingerbread-looking stone house to the left of ours. I'd seen people staying there on occasion during the summer, usually groups of young adults who partied too loud and pissed my parents off. They never would have agreed to live in Hillendale year-round, even if dad's factory job were closer. *It's a place for summer, not for a real life,* they would say. And I often got the impression that they looked down on the permanent families, at least the ones who lived full-time in the small cottages and rentals.

"Are you living year-round then?" my mother asked them, hiding her judgement well.

The woman smiled. I liked her name better than her daughter's. *Isabella.* A pretty name.

"That's the plan. It's just Kathi Jo and I. I love to kayak, and I used to live here with my family on the other side of the lake. Being here feels like home."

"Willow, why don't you take a walk with Kathi Jo, let us grown-ups talk? You can show her the path down to the lake in case she likes to go swimming," my mother said.

I could barely conceal my amusement. Covering my mouth with my hand, I glanced over at Kathi Jo; she wiggled both brows, the corner of her lips hinting at a smile.

"Sure. Why not? Do you like to go swimming?" I asked.

"Definitely," Kathi Jo said, grinning. She had a nice smile, like something out of a magazine.

Our mothers were watching as we high-tailed it through the kitchen, snaking through the slide-in screen off the back porch.

Kathi Jo burst into giggles as soon as we stepped outside. I held up one finger to my lips. Dad was somewhere nearby.

"Morning, there!" Dad said.

Kathi Jo startled, and I squeezed her arm jovially, snorting with glee.

"Morning, Dad. Just going for a walk with our new neighbor." Dad was sprawled out in a plastic deck chair, his feet propped up on the seat of another chair, his cup of decaf in one hand and a Clancy paperback in the other.

"We have neighbors?" he asked, flicking a page. His eyes were red, and he looked hung over.

"Yep." Kathi Jo and I brushed past him, heading for the woods. I led the way, curling around the behemoth rock, brushing it for luck on my way by.

I glanced back just in time to see Kathi Jo doing the same.

As we skirted through the woods, I was sweating. Even with the canopy of trees overhead, I could tell the sun was going to be reckless today. By the end of summer, the grass would be crunchy and brown beneath my feet, my skin tanned dark as leather before returning to school in Branton.

We waited until we had reached the clearing and were out of earshot, before speaking.

Kathi Jo laughed so hard she had to bend at the waist. I kicked off my sneakers and socks, chuckling too.

"First time seeing the lake, huh?" I teased.

"First time during the daytime, I guess," Kathi Jo said. "Why did you ignore me last night when I called out to you? I could see you there on the balcony, plain as day. Were you pretending to be asleep?"

A flutter of shame tickled my belly, remembering how embarrassed I'd felt last night. I shook it off, again reminding myself that she was the one caught skinny-dipping like a midnight maiden.

I told the truth: "I don't know why. You just surprised me is all … and I wasn't sure how to react. To be honest, I thought maybe you were some sort of sea creature. A goddess of the night…"

"Goddess of the night, eh? That's a little dramatic." Kathi Jo slipped off her flip-flops and took one step toward the water.

I blushed. "I'm a writer. I guess my imagination runs away with me sometimes."

Instead of moving on to another subject or teasing me about writing, Kathi Jo raised her eyebrows with interest.

"A writer? That's pretty amazing."

"Do you write, too?"

Kathi Jo shook her head. "No, but I like to read. Maybe I can read your stories one day." She stretched one foot out, making a slow rippled circle in the water.

"So you like to read, and you like to go swimming naked at midnight," I chaffed, lowering myself to the edge of the water beside her.

"Yes. Why not?" she said, giddily.

For a few moments everything was quiet, just two strangers with our feet in the water, cooking under the summer sun. I had so many questions. How old was she? How did she feel about living in this tiny lake town year-round? Why did they move here from the other side of the lake? And where did she get that tattoo and those strange piercings?

I was trying to decide which to ask first, when Kathi Jo leaned in close, shadows dancing in the hollows of her cheeks. Her lips brushed against my ear.

"Want to see a dead body?" she whispered.

The Summer She Disappeared:
Chapter 2

Can you keep a secret?

CURRENT DAY

The lake house was like stepping through the Looking Glass in Alice in Wonderland, everything hazy and distorted. Of course, I'd been inside since returning to town, but now things were … different.

The dead animals on the walls had been taken down by Cindy and the rest of the crew. The old-timey red drapes that clashed with the lime green paint were gone; bundled up in a corner of the room, like a bloody tumor. I stood in the doorway, Cindy breathing down my neck, unable to force my legs to move closer to the bedroom.

When I found out the lake house was mine, it couldn't

have come at a better time. Jason was the breadwinner in our marriage, his salary as a principal dwarfed my meager part-time earnings from teaching; so, when I filed for divorce, there was no doubt that I would be the one leaving. I couldn't afford the mortgage on our 300k house; I could barely afford the cheap apartment I was renting across the lake while I waited on these renovations to finish up.

But my inheritance from my parents offered me a new solution: I could either sell the lake house for a decent profit —houses here were worth much more than they used to be when my parents were my age now—or I could keep it as a rental property, using the money as an extra source of steady income while I figured out what to do about teaching and where to live.

There was a third option: staying in Hillendale, keeping the house for myself. But I certainly didn't want to do that. There were good memories here, but also ugly ones.

Hillendale, albeit a small town, was a great investment these days, according to my realtor. People rented out houses and cottages here every summer, some of them for upward of $500–1,000 per night. City people with money were dying for a slice of the "rugged" life, nestled in this small Kentucky lakeside town. Although the houses here weren't at all what I would consider "rugged".

I'd allowed the realtor to pressure me a bit, finally, taking out a home improvement loan to do the repairs on the lake house. *If you're going to rent it out, or even sell it, you need to do it right. Maximize your profits*, the realtor had explained. She was right about the house needing improvements: it had sat empty for years, our days of family visits and vacations long gone.

The whole house had that unused smell about it—damp and musty, like the inside of a sealed-up tomb. It needed a lot of work, inside and out. Landscaping, concrete patio repairs, gutters, carpet…

More work than I'd initially expected.

Most of my visits had been short and sweet, checking on the state of repairs and collaborating with the company I'd hired to do the job. The past few weeks, their work has mostly been done on the exterior.

But tonight, here I was … stepping inside it, moving back through time…

The house was a maze—scaffolding in the living room, buckets of unopened paint, tools, and ladders clogging up every open space and pathway.

I forced myself onward, putting one foot in front of the other, snaking around the crew's equipment.

"It's in there," Cindy said, her voice raw like she'd just been screaming. I flinched at the sound of it; I'd nearly forgotten she was behind me.

"Which room?"

She pointed down the long dark hallway that led to the main bedroom, the one my parents slept in every summer when we came to the lake.

"Wait." I turned around to look at Cindy. In the low-lit living room, I could see her face, the pallor of her skin almost green. As I stepped closer to her, I caught a whiff of something sour, perhaps vomit on her clothes.

"What were you doing here this late, Cindy?" It was an important question, but nothing that couldn't have waited until after I looked at what was in that bedroom. But I needed to know; her late-night presence here was not only unusual, but it was also unnerving and unprofessional.

Cindy stammered, "I-I…"

"It's okay. I just want to know why."

Cindy lowered her eyes. "I had a row with my husband. A bad one, worse than usual. I live over in Greenville, you know?"

I nodded, although I wasn't as familiar with Hillendale or its neighboring towns as I should have been. Greenville wasn't far, I did know that; just a short commute for her to the site each day.

"I didn't know where else to go, and I tend to focus on my work when I'm upset. I love breaking shit when I'm pissed."

"Breaking shit?"

"Yeah, that's why I brought my sledgehammer. We're going to knock down the wall between the master and the spare, create a walk-in closet, yeah?" Cindy said.

"Yeah." My head was spinning. I couldn't remember all that was on the agenda; and with whatever was going on now, none of it probably mattered anymore.

"I started smashing and it felt good. I figured the guys wouldn't mind me getting an early start … but then I stopped for a smoke break. And…"

"And?"

"And while I was smoking, I took a look around the rooms. I wanted to size them up, get a feel for what it would look like when we were done. That's when I opened the closet," Cindy said.

With that, there was no more time for stalling. Slowly, I entered the hallway, eyes focused on the room at its very end.

The door was open, the room casting an orange, ghostly glow from within. For a moment, I could almost imagine my parents in there: Dad on the left side of the bed with his reading glasses, working a crossword; Mom on the right, buffing her nails, hair twisted up in rollers as part of her nighttime routine.

But when I stepped inside there was nothing, just an empty room. The bed and the nightstands were gone. My parents were gone. And the door to the bedroom closet was open.

"Did you call the police?" I asked Cindy, breathlessly, frozen six feet away from the closet.

"No. I wanted to call you first."

It seemed like a strange reaction, but I was grateful she had called me. I had to see this for myself. Had to see if it was real.

As I approached the closet, I could sense that Cindy was no longer behind me. When I glanced back, she was hovering in the doorway, bracing her hands on the frame.

I took a breath and stepped closer. There was no lighting in the closet. A memory came out of nowhere: Mom bitching that Dad was too lazy to install a light fixture and she had to reach in blind for her clothes. That was around the time the fighting started…

All of Mom's summer clothes were gone now—the shirts and shorts, the flimsy summer dresses, and jumpers… All that remained was a long metal bar and a handful of dingy, wire hangers.

And the long black dress bag on the floor of the closet.

I knew without opening it that that was where the body was. The bag obviously contained something solid, the sides bulging. The shape of shoulders and … and a head.

"You zipped it back up after?" I said, flabbergasted, looking back at Cindy.

"Yeah. I couldn't… I didn't want to see those eyes anymore," her voice shook.

Squatting down on my haunches, I reached for the slim black zipper at the top of the bag.

"Wait. Maybe we shouldn't touch it anymore… Maybe we should call and wait for someone to…"

But it was too late to go back now. I couldn't wait another second. I had to see whose body was inside that bag.

Cindy made a strange gurgling noise as I tugged the zipper all the way down, exposing the secrets within.

~

SUMMER OF '98

"Can you keep a secret?" Kathi Jo asked.

We had borrowed her mother's banana yellow kayak. Although I'd offered to take a turn, Kathi Jo held tightly to the oars, rowing farther and farther from the bank. Our houses grew smaller and smaller as she rowed us further into the lake.

I was surprised my mom had agreed to it; I was only thirteen and she never let me swim in the water without her keeping a watchful eye. But Kathi Jo's mother had jumped in with a "yes" before my mother could respond, and as it turned out, Kathi Jo was a year older than me; she was fourteen. *She's an excellent swimmer. I'm sure they won't go far;* Isabella had reassured my mother, of which I was grateful.

"I can keep a secret," I said. Scooting forward on the hard yellow seat, we were so close our knees were touching.

Kathi Jo had mentioned a body. That had to be some sort of joke, right?

"I found bones in the basement when we moved in, in this tiny little nook in the wall. At first, I thought they were plastic, some sort of Halloween shit left behind. But then … I touched them. They weren't props, that's for sure. Something terrible happened in that house," Kathi Jo said.

A chill ran from the base of my neck all the way down the length of my spine. My family had vacationed here every summer since I could remember—how many times had I played close to the house next door? I'd never gone inside it. But there were times when I'd been afraid that someone was in there, looking out the windows, watching when it was supposed to be empty…

"What kind of bones?" I asked.

Kathi Jo held the oar steady. I stared at the chipped black polish on her nails.

"Some of them could be animal bones. It's hard to know for certain. But one of them is clearly a jawbone ... I'm starting to think maybe it's a full body, the skeleton in pieces..."

So, that's what she meant by wanting to see a "body".

"What did your mom say about it?"

Kathi Jo shook her head solemnly. "I didn't tell her."

"What! Why?" Sometimes I couldn't stand my mom and Dad, but if I found a body—or bones—in the house, I sure as shit would run screaming for them.

"I knew she'd call the cops and then they'd take them. Or worse, they'd take our whole house. Mom just bought this place. I don't want to move again ... not after all the stuff with my dad..." Kathi Jo said.

Kathi Jo stopped rowing and bit her lip. It was a nervous tic, that over time, I'd come to recognize and find endearing.

Two things struck me then about Kathi Jo: she hadn't had an easy life, and she was the bravest person I knew. I couldn't imagine finding random bones in my new basement and keeping that all to myself.

"So, what are you going to do?" I asked. It came out louder than I'd intended, my voice echoing across the fog-covered lake, bouncing back and forth through the trees. I prayed our mothers weren't sitting out back, overhearing everything. Sound really travels on water.

"Not me. *Us.* Now that you know the secret, what are we going to do? How are we going to solve this?" Kathi Jo asked.

ONE MORE CHAPTER

One More Chapter is an
award-winning global
division of HarperCollins.

Sign up to our newsletter to get our
latest eBook deals and stay up to date
with our weekly Book Club!
<u>Subscribe here.</u>

Meet the team at
<u>www.onemorechapter.com</u>

Follow us!
 @OneMoreChapter_
 @OneMoreChapter
 @onemorechapterhc

Do you write unputdownable fiction?
We love to hear from new voices.
Find out how to submit your novel at
<u>www.onemorechapter.com/submissions</u>